FOR THE LOVE C̲ ̲.̲.̲.̲.̲.̲.̲

By

Margaret Brazear

https://www.margaret-brazear.com

TABLE OF CONTENTS

CHAPTER ONE
Home to Hever

Nobody asked Anne if she wanted to go home to Hever Castle; her father, Sir Thomas Boleyn, ordered her back to England to marry, she knew not who, not until she arrived home to see her mother, who greeted her with a smile and a quick hug.

"He is James Butler, who will one day be the ninth Earl of Ormond," said her mother. "Your distant cousin in Ireland. You will be his countess. Tis a good match and it will settle a dispute that has long caused a breach in our family."

Ireland? She had been educated in the elegant court of France, had friends among the French nobility. It was well known that Ireland was a wild and brutal land, wet and cold and savage.

Anne's dark eyes fixed on her mother's face for a few seconds before she replied.

"Why should I be used to settle a dispute?" she said. "I have grown to womanhood in the court of France; I do not want to wither away in some Irish wasteland."

Her mother's smile disappeared and she glared at her daughter as though wanting to freeze her with a look.

"You'll do as you are told," she said. "The King himself has sanctioned the marriage. Indeed, he has commanded it."

The news that she was to wed this stranger made Anne's longing to be back in France even more urgent, more painful.

She had friends in France as well as servants she trusted and she had been there so long it was her home; she had no wish to leave it. Her hope had been that a match would be found for her from among the French courtiers so that she could stay there. She barely remembered how to speak English.

But war had once again broken out between England and France, so leave it she must and she was given little time at home, at Hever Castle, before she was presented at the English court. There she was a stranger without friends, without even a familiar face to soothe her fears. Her sister, Mary, had been at court, but was now married with children.

There were rumours about Mary, that she had been the King's mistress, now discarded by him. The children might well not be her husband's, might be of the King's making. People looked askance at Anne because of Mary. She even heard a whispered mention of 'the whore's sister' as she passed an open door and that made her angry. She saw no just reason that she should be condemned because of Mary's lack of morals and she was not about to tolerate it.

She pushed open the door and stepped inside, where she saw two ladies at their embroidery. Both looked up, startled to see her there.

"I am newly come to court," said Anne. "I know nothing of what went before but be assured, I am not my sister."

Then she spun around and left them open mouthed, regretting that they had ever judged Mistress Boleyn.

But Anne was no fool and she could easily see where her family stood in the eyes of the King. Sir Thomas had a good position among his courtiers, but that position could disappear as quickly as a snap of the royal fingers. Perhaps Mary had little choice; Anne hoped that was the way of things.

Festivities were loud and colourful when Anne appeared in the great hall at the palace. Ladies showed off their colourful and beautiful gowns as they danced, the gentlemen no less so. But colour did not make style and Anne realised her own apparel was not like that worn here, that her French style of dress soon attracted the attention of the other ladies.

Such attention did not frighten Anne; she was accustomed to admiration from French courtiers and even the King of France himself, but her own attention was on the young men. Her mother had told her that her betrothed, James Butler, might well be at the palace on occasion as he was a member of Cardinal Wolsey's household. Anne was anxious to see what he looked like at least. If she could meet him before the marriage, she might know what manner of man he was and if he could be persuaded to live in England instead of the wilds of Ireland.

She wondered if her mother had forgotten what it was for a maiden to want to see pleasing features, to want a handsome man and one whose personal habits were of a pleasant nature.

The great Cardinal was absent from this first banquet, but there were many young men eager to make themselves known to her. And, just as in France, she could not fail to notice that the women were not so friendly.

She had been at court for some few days when she had word that the Cardinal would be visiting with his entourage and she took great care with her appearance, for if she was anxious to be pleased with her betrothed's looks, she thought it likely that he might feel the same about her.

Anne knew she was not particularly beautiful. She had almost black hair and eyes to match, but those eyes were a little wider than she would have chosen. Her lips were full and she held her head high as a necessity, to straighten her neck and show off the many necklets she liked to wear, like the velvet band and a close circle of pearls.

On this occasion she wore beautiful cornflour blue satin with a French hood to match. The colour suited her dark hair and eyes very well and made them stand out in all their beauty.

She wondered, as she gazed at her reflection, if she were really dressing to please her betrothed, or whether there was some other motive, one she could not acknowledge. Was she, perhaps, dressing for herself, or even for other gentlemen about the court? She had always attracted attention; at the French court she had been a great favourite among the courtiers who flocked to her side whenever she appeared. It was perfectly natural that she should expect such attention here, at the English court.

It could hardly go unnoticed that Anne's style of dress, her French hoods and her fur trimmed, long sleeves, had been lately taken up by other ladies about the court.

Anne wondered what she would do if James Butler proved to be hideous in her eyes. She wondered how she would avoid a marriage with him, a marriage that the King himself had ordered, and not being able to avoid such a state, how she would live with a man she could not admire and respect. Those things were important to her, very important, and unlike many other ladies of her status, she was determined to keep herself for her husband. Not for her any brief and sordid affairs, no matter the temptation.

Her thoughts were interrupted by a loud knock on the door.

"Mistress Boleyn," a voice called. "'Tis past time. If you do not arrive before their majesties, you'll miss your meal."

Her heart jumped nervously. Perhaps missing her meal would not be such a bad thing on this occasion, but no; she might as well get it over with.

She followed the palace servant through what seemed like endless galleries to the banqueting hall. It was a magnificent hall, the ceiling lined with canvas paintings of scenes from history and gold paint to add to the decoration.

Anne took her seat for what proved to be a sumptuous meal, but there was no sign of the Cardinal or his household. Of course, he would not be here at the banquet; he would arrive later, if at all.

Anne observed the royal couple throughout the meal, casting surreptitious glances their way whenever she thought she might not be observed. The King was a heavy man, tall and slightly overweight, and judging by the amount of food he shoved into his mouth, it would soon be more than slight. He was athletic, to be sure, so perhaps his physical activity would counteract his overeating.

Anne had heard, while she was in France, that the King of England was a handsome man, but she really could not see it. He was striking, it was true, being so tall and muscular, but his features were not pleasing, at least not in her eyes.

His eyes were too small, as was his mouth, and his large face appeared even larger because of it.

He was richly dressed, as one would expect, in purple velvet studded with precious stones and his red hair peeked out from beneath a matching velvet cap with a feather for extra decoration.

Queen Katherine was also richly dressed, but she looked dour somehow, as though not enjoying this extravagance. She was duty bound to be here if the King commanded it, but Anne sensed that she would rather have stayed quiet in her chambers. And it seemed to Anne that she was not alone in casting surreptitious glances at the King. Katherine, too was watching and from what Anne had heard, it was likely that lady watched to see on whom her husband's eyes would rest.

Anne wondered what it must be like, to be a royal princess and Queen to a man who could not stay faithful, one who thought it is his right to spread his favours around every woman to whom he took a fancy.

Katherine had to remain loyal to him, no matter how much he hurt her with his philandering. She had to pretend it was not happening and behave like the Queen she was.

In the past, Queen Katherine had earned the King's respect and trust and was given regency over the nation when he was away. But it seemed likely she no longer held that trust, that he had grown away from her in recent years. It was sad that a couple who had once loved each other, now after some twenty years had little in common and that he turned elsewhere for comfort.

Anne would never tolerate such infidelity from a husband of hers; she would fight to keep him at her side, no matter what it took. She might be promised to an Irish nobleman she had yet to meet, she might be condemned to the wilds of Ireland, but she would not want to swap places with Queen Katherine just the same.

The Queen was older than her husband, although not by many years, but she looked much older now. Perhaps it was the strain of constantly worrying about producing a son for him, perhaps it was not Henry but those stillborn sons who had broken her heart. Or it could have been the death of her baby boy, Henry, who lived only seven weeks.

How horrible, to hold that child in her arms, to love him, to fill her heart with him, only to have him snatched away. That must have devastated her after the celebrations and the joy of a young prince, an heir to the throne.

Katherine had once been lovely, with soft, plump cheeks and pretty auburn hair, not dark as one would expect of a Spaniard. Indeed she had been very comely when first she came to court to wed this King's brother.

She had been through a lot since then. It was said that the last King kept her short of everything when his son, Arthur, died and left her a widow. She had certainly not been treated as an important royal princess. She had even been short of basic needs like food for years until Henry VII died and his son succeeded to the throne as well as to his late brother's widow.

Now it seemed that after so many years of happiness, she was once again to be disrespected. It was sad and Anne decided there and then that she did not like this King and she would never want to be a Queen if this was what it meant.

Anne had been dancing with a young man whose name she had forgotten when the Cardinal finally arrived. Ladies curtsied, men bowed as the man hurried to the King and knelt at his feet. He was completely covered in red, his cloak, his hood, even his gloves. Anne wondered if he expected an outbreak of smallpox, as doctors had declared that wearing the colour red would ward off the disease.

But her eyes wandered past the great churchman to his pages, the young men who followed him, and wondered which one might be James Butler.

There was one among them who caught her eye. He was very handsome, with dark hair and a nicely trimmed beard. He had a good figure as well, the figure of a man who enjoyed sports of all kinds.

But what attracted Anne more than all that was the mischievous smile and the twinkling, dark eyes. She smiled back, then turned away to hide it. If this was her betrothed, she would have no complaint.

She thought it must be him, as he was so blatant in the way he flirted with her from across the room. Surely only a man with a claim would behave so.

She was so fixed on this young man, she did not even notice another young man who appeared beside her and bowed.

"Mistress Boleyn," he said. "Allow me to present myself. I am James Butler."

Her heart sank but she forced a smile and turned to face him. He was not nearly so handsome as the one whom she had first noticed. His face was heavier, his nose large and his beard full and bushy, brown like his curly hair. He was not overweight, not in any extreme way at any rate. His teeth were even and no evil smells came from either his breath or his body.

But there was no mischief in his eyes and his smile was absent altogether. A serious man, perhaps, one who would expect no gaiety in his house, no laughter. But perhaps she misjudged him; perhaps he was only hesitant to introduce himself in this company for fear of her reaction.

She curtsied quickly and held out her hand for him to kiss.

"I am pleased to meet you, Sir," she said.

"And I you," he replied. "It seems we are promised to each other. I hope that suits you."

A sharp retort sprang to her tongue, but she forced it back. She doubted Mr Butler had any more say in matters than she did herself.

"I hope it does too," she said at last. "Perhaps we should dance."

"I do not dance," he said. "It is not a skill that is needed in Ireland. At least, not this sort of dancing."

"What sort is that?"

"A little formal for my taste," he said. "Irish dancing is more vigorous and carefree."

"In that case," said a new voice, "perhaps you'll not object if the lady dances with me."

James glanced at the newcomer and shook his head slightly. It was the handsome young man with the mischievous smile.

"Harry," he said. "I guessed you'd not be far away."

"Please," said the man called Harry. "Introduce me."

"Very well. Mistress Anne Boleyn, may I present my colleague, Lord Harry Percy, heir to the Earldom of Northumberland and too important for his own good."

James Butler seemed happy enough to step aside and allow Lord Percy to dance with his betrothed. They danced till past midnight, till the King himself ended things by leaving the hall.

The following day, she was called to the Queen's chambers and told she was to be a maid of honour to Her Majesty.

CHAPTER TWO
The Love of Her Life

Anne was pleased to have been chosen as a member of the Queen's household, but she found the company somewhat dull. The Queen and her ladies embroidered a lot, and sang, and gossiped but most of all they prayed as Queen Katherine was a very pious woman. She insisted on mass twice a day for all her ladies and the rattle of rosaries and the constant crossing of oneself made Anne very uncomfortable.

When she could do so unobserved, she had spent a lot of time studying the works of Martin Luther and his new ideas about religion. She knew that would be regarded as heresy, so she said nothing, but she was finding the strict Catholic dogma in the Queen's household to be tedious in the extreme. Anne could not simply follow it all and believe, she needed to question, but she dared not question aloud.

What brightened her evenings was that Cardinal Wolsey often visited the King and when he did so, his page, one Lord Harry Percy, tarried in the Queen's apartments with her ladies. One in particular caught his eye, that same Mistress Boleyn he had met before, but now they spent much time whispering in corners and laughing together.

That was the start of it and, as well as their evenings in the Queen's company, they often met alone, in the same spot, a clearing among the trees in the palace grounds. Unless anyone was particularly looking, they would not be noticed, although they had no reason to keep their meetings secret. They talked. Anne told him about her life in France, at the French court, about how much she loved the Queen of that country. Harry talked about his childhood in Northumberland, about how he had been groomed to be the very important and illustrious Earl of that county when his father died.

Their blossoming love for one another meant everything to them and they just wanted to keep it to themselves for a little while, before consent needed to be sought from his father and hers, before their elders got involved and tried to arrange everything.

"That Butler chap thinks you are to marry him," he said. "You're not, are you?"

"Not if I have a say. My father is in dispute about the title, thinks it should be his. I am supposed to calm things."

"They have promised me to the daughter of the Earl of Shrewsbury," he told her. "Her name is Mary, Mary Talbot, but I shall refuse to marry her if you say you will have me."

They were lying together beneath an oak tree. They had been just lying there, looking up at the clouds, and wishing this could go on forever.

Her eyes sparkled as they met his, as they searched his face to be sure he spoke the truth. Then she reached for him, held him close to her and kissed him. Those kisses were something she had never known before and they aroused feelings in her she could never have imagined. She wanted to feel him against her, feel his body close to hers, wanted to feel that final test of love that she had heard about.

"Yes, I will have you Harry Percy. I love you."

"And I love you. We must hold out against the promises made by our fathers. James Butler is wanting to take you to Ireland."

She shook her head.

"I'll not go," she said. "I suppose we must ask the King for his consent."

"I suppose so; and the Cardinal."

"I was told the King had commanded my marriage, although I have no idea why he would have an interest." A sudden fear clutched at her heart and she leaned in closer to him, held him even tighter. "Oh, Harry," she said. "What will we do if they refuse?"

"We will elope," he said. "We will run away together and live in a wooden hut."

"Will we, Harry? Do you promise?"

"I promise."

He kissed her then, held her so tight she could scarcely breathe and she felt that unfamiliar throbbing deep inside, that need that was as powerful as hunger or thirst.

They had no idea they were being observed.

***

Cardinal Wolsey listened carefully to the young page. He was a rather unpleasant young fellow, named Clarence, the sort of person who was always trying to be first with the gossip so as to make himself important. But still, his latest piece might well be worth hearing. It seemed it was, as Clarence related every detail of the conversation he had overheard.

Wolsey knew something that young Clarence did not, that nobody else knew. The King himself had told him that he had his eye on Mistress Boleyn and he was to be sure her planned marriage to James Butler did not happen.

Wolsey was sure the King would be just as eager for this association with Lord Percy to be stopped and the King's reaction to the news proved him right.

"They must be separated, at all costs," ordered the King.

Wolsey's purpose in life was to please King Henry and this was no different. He knew that Percy's father, the Earl of Northumberland, would likely refuse his consent, even without the King's interference, so it should not be too difficult.

He would not send for young Percy. He would wait for their evening meal, where he could best display his authority and make his opinions clear.

When Harry arrived in the Cardinal's hall at Westminster that evening, his head was full of Anne and the love they had for each other. He hated to leave her this evening, wanted to take her to his bed and make love to her, wanted to satisfy his need for her. He had no space among his thoughts for anything else and he failed to notice the silence that fell over the company when he appeared.

It was not until he approached the dais and noticed the angry gaze of his employer that he realised something was very wrong, although what, he could not have guessed. Perhaps someone had died; Harry could think of nothing else that would account for such a sombre atmosphere.

"Ah, Lord Percy," said the Cardinal. "Thank you for joining us. I hear you have been very much engaged with entertaining young Mistress Boleyn."

Harry's eyes met his defiantly. What he wanted to do was ask Wolsey what the hell his love life had to do with him, but he knew that it had everything to do with him. Yet to ask about his private business here, among the whole household, was crass and ignorant in Harry's opinion. What more could one expect of a man of such low beginnings? Who was he to treat him like this? Nothing but the son of a butcher.

"As it happens, Your Grace," he replied, "you are correct. Anne and I are betrothed and wish to be married as soon as may be."

"Do you indeed?" said Wolsey. "Well, you need to remember your place, young man, as well as your duty to your family."

"What does that mean? My duty to my family involves marrying and procuring an heir. That is what I intend to do."

"Not with Mistress Boleyn," said the Cardinal. "You are promised elsewhere, and you know it. She too is promised elsewhere. Your father's consent to this ill favoured match will not be forthcoming, neither will mine. I very much think the King himself will have a say."

"The King? Anne wondered why he had commanded her marriage."

"The King commanded her marriage to settle a long standing family dispute. He'll not be happy to have his wishes ignored. Your choice is not good enough for the son of one of the most important and wealthy earldoms in the kingdom."

Harry was furious. He looked about him at the staring eyes, all firmly fixed on him. There were even some sniggers from his colleagues, yet he found no opinion in the countenance of James Butler. He stood silent, his eyes and expression showing nothing of how he felt about this abuse to his position as Anne's betrothed.

Harry had no time to consider what that meant; he had to reclaim his dignity in whatever way he could.

"Anne might well be the daughter of a mere knight," he said. "But her mother is the daughter of the Duke of Norfolk. She is easily my equal."

"The King has forbidden it," said Wolsey.

That was when Harry felt tears gathering in his throat. If the King had, for whatever reason, forbidden it, there was nothing he could do. He was going to lose Anne and he was certain he would never recover from that loss.

"Surely the King will relent when he knows how much we love each other," said Harry. "I am convinced my father can be persuaded."

"We will see when he gets here," said the Cardinal. "I have sent for him."

Wolsey knew for certain that the Earl of Northumberland, Harry's father, would refuse his consent because Wolsey would make sure of it. Once he knew the match found no favour with the King, he would have no choice other than to refuse. What no one must know was that the King himself had a fancy to take young Mistress Boleyn to his bed.

He had already known one sister; why not the other?

***

Anne waited for over an hour in their secret meeting place, but Harry never came. She knew well he would not have let her down if he had a choice, so something must have happened to keep him from her. It must have been something to do with his duties for the Cardinal, something he could not avoid, but knowing all that did nothing to ease her disappointment.

Fighting back tears, she told herself firmly that he would be here tomorrow. He would not disappoint her two days in a row; he might even have sent a note. It could be waiting for her in her suite. Now the sun was moving across the sky and she needed to get back to her own apartment before she was missed.

It was not a note from Harry that awaited her; it was her father. That was unusual, strange even; he never visited her. But he was visiting her now and he did not look pleased.

"Father," she said. "This is an unexpected honour."

"Unexpected? It should most certainly be expected, since you have seen fit to entangle yourself with young Harry Percy without my consent, nor the King's."

Anne caught her breath. It was only yesterday that she and Harry had pledged themselves to each other; gossip travelled fast in court circles, but not this fast, surely. Someone must have gone out of their way to tell Sir Thomas of his daughter's betrothal and she had a good idea who that someone might be. The butcher's son, Wolsey, he who believed it was his place to interfere in the lives of his betters.

"You should be pleased, Father," she said. "He is the heir to Northumberland, not a minor earldom like Ormond."

"You stupid girl!" he shouted. "You'll never be allowed to marry into that family, you, a mere nobody and just when I was beginning to gain some favour with the King. You have likely lost me my title."

"You have no title."

"Not now, no, but I would have."

Anne bit back a retort, but it would not stay hidden. She was angry and her temper had ever had a will of its own.

"Still enjoying the spoils of whoring out your daughter?" she said.

She did not see the blow coming; it was too sudden, too fast, but she certainly felt the sting. Holding her cheek to soothe it, she stepped back and fought against the tears that sprang up.

"You are to return to Hever, at once," he said.

"No. I will marry Harry. I love him."

"Harry Percy is confined to his chamber while he awaits the arrival of his father. He'll likely take him back to Northumberland; he cannot stay here now."

She shook her head, still clutching her injured face.

"I want to see him," she said.

His mouth turned down in a grimace, as though disgusted with her and he likely was.

"You are even more stupid than I thought," he said. "Nobody is going to let you see him ever again. The sooner you get over him and let him concentrate on his marriage, the sooner we can all get back to normal."

"His marriage?" she said. "His marriage to a girl he's never met, one he does not want? He wants me! We love each other."

He clucked his tongue and shook his head, flung open her clothes chest and let the lid bounce against the bedpost.

"Have your things packed. We leave in an hour."

She watched him go, then a maidservant came in to pack her boxes for the journey to Kent. Anne sat in the window seat and stared out at the beautiful palace gardens, her memory full of Harry's promises. He would not let anyone stop them; they would elope, run away together and be married. But where was he now?

Anne knew well he would be here to keep his promise had they not locked him up to wait to be taken home to Northumberland in disgrace. It would be a week or more before his father could get here, but Anne would have no chance to sneak in and see Harry. She would be in Kent, waiting for a marriage to a stiff and silent Irishman who likely wanted her no more than she wanted him.

What did it matter? Without Harry, nothing mattered. It made no difference if she were in Ireland or in London, she would be just as miserable, just as lonely.

Sir Thomas came back to see if she was ready to leave, another personal touch she had never before encountered.

"You are packed?" he asked.

She stared at him defiantly.

"I'll not marry the Irishman," she said. "And Harry'll not wed Mary Talbot."

"He will if the King commands it," he answered. "That or lose his head."

"He is no traitor!"

"Defying King Henry is not a wise choice. He'll find something to twist it into treason if he so wishes and you should be thankful. His Majesty has taken a particular interest in your wellbeing."

She made no reply. If he spoke the truth, Anne knew well his meaning, but she would not go the way of her sister. All at once she was glad to be leaving court.

CHAPTER THREE
Do Not Tell Mary

"Do not tell Mary."

Mary Talbot was not a listener at doors. She always assumed that if a subject involved her, she would be told about it. But to hear her father's voice through a half open doorway, demanding a secret be kept from her – that was a different matter.

She stopped and pushed the door open wider. No doubt her father would not be happy to know that she had overheard, but she could not concern herself with that.

"Do not tell Mary what?" she demanded.

The Earl of Shrewsbury turned from his conversation with his secretary and looked at her for only a few seconds before he spoke.

"Now you have spoilt the surprise," he said. "I was going to announce it at the banquet on Saturday."

"Announce what? If it concerns me, I should be at least included in the arrangements."

"Forgive me," said the Earl. It was a few minutes before he went on, hoping his daughter might prefer to be surprised, but she made no move to leave the room. "The fact is, your marriage to Lord Harry Percy has been brought forward. You are to wed early in the new year."

"Why? Surely he has another two years or more with the Cardinal before he can marry."

"His father has decided to take him home and train him to inherit the title when he dies. I know nothing more."

Mary did not believe him, but if he thought she would mildly obey his wishes and accept his word, he was mistaken. She knew how important Percy's time in the Cardinal's household was and she thought it unlikely that his father would take him away from that, not unless he found himself terminally ill.

Mary had a friend at court, Lady Lucinda Hampton, a maid of honour to Queen Katherine. She would write to her at once, hope to receive an answer to the conundrum before the banquet.

Nothing more was said about the sudden change and Mary watched the servants, hurrying to get the banquet ready for Saturday. It was a regular thing, a celebration for the local gentry, nothing exceptional. She felt sure her father was using it as an excuse to announce her forthcoming marriage.

Once the date was announced, it would give the betrothal a more official seal than it had so far had, so the urgency she felt was understandable. She had begun to give up hope of a reply before the announcement when it arrived, a sealed letter from Lucinda in London.

My Dearest Friend, it read, *I was both surprised and perturbed at your request for information concerning your betrothed. I assumed you would know more about matters than I, but if your noble father has seen fit to bring forward the date of your marriage to Lord Percy, I believe you have a right to know what has been going on here.*

My dear, there has been a terrible scandal. Harry Percy has seen fit to betroth himself to a girl of no consequence, one Mistress Anne Boleyn, the daughter of a mere knight. Tis true her mother is a Howard, but her father comes from low stock. The pair declared themselves to be in love, if you please.

Harry Percy has been sent home in disgrace, as has the girl. She too was promised elsewhere, although what is happening about that I cannot tell.

The Cardinal upbraided him before his entire household and words were spoken which can never be forgiven. I believe Lord Percy informed His Grace, Cardinal Wolsey, that he was nothing more than a butcher's son and had no right to speak to him so. One has to be amused at the audacity of the man.

Either way, I believe this is the reason for your sudden change in circumstance. I am so sorry, my dear. I am sure that once he sees his beautiful bride, young Harry will soon forget his feelings for Mistress Boleyn.

I am sorry to be the one to tell you, my dear friend, but it is a fact that Lord Percy's father, the Earl of Northumberland, came here himself and warned Harry that he had two more sons and that if Harry did not obey him and marry where he was promised, he would disinherit him and leave everything to one of his brothers.

It is rumoured that the reason permission was refused is because the King himself has cast his eyes on Mistress Boleyn, but how much truth there is in that, I cannot say for certain.

Forever your friend and obedient servant,
Lucinda Hampton

Mary crunched the letter up in her fist and moved to the window to look out and see that her father was there, discussing something with a man she had never before seen. She wondered if he was some emissary from the Earl of Northumberland, come to arrange her life for her.

Well, she would have none of it! It was bad enough to be duty bound to wed a man she had never met, but to wed a man who was in love with someone else was too demeaning to even think about.

She left her bedchamber and hurried down the stairs, out into the grounds and toward her father who had turned away from his visitor. His expression seemed to take on a sort of forced joy when he saw his daughter, not a smile of greeting and pleasure, but one that he had deliberately put upon his face.

"Mary, my dear," he said. "How lovely. Not long now till the banquet tonight and my announcement of your official betrothal. Are you not excited?"

"Is that what I am supposed to be?" she replied. She waved the letter at him. "I have word from a friend at court. She tells me my future husband has declared himself in love with another woman, has even promised her marriage."

The false smile fell from his face to be replaced with a pink flush.

"It is true he has disgraced himself," he said. "I'll not deny it."

"You would have denied it had I not already the proof." Mary's voice rose as she settled her fist around the crunched up letter. "You care nothing for me, for my happiness. You want to tie me to a man who will never respect me, who will resent me for not being someone else."

The Earl stiffened. He had no experience of his daughter arguing with him, of her not obeying him without question. He was angry, yes, but he had to soothe her fears or this whole situation could turn to disaster.

"You'll obey me, Mary, if you please. I have always had your best interests at heart, as you well know. This situation is no exception. Lord Percy obviously had an infatuation for this girl, which he was not entitled to have, but that is all it was, an infatuation. He knows where his duty lies, as do you."

"My duty does not extend to marrying a man who will always consider me to be second best."

"I'm afraid it does, my dear." He paused and drew a deep breath to settle his temper. "I blame the Cardinal for this. He was supposed to be supervising the pages in his household, not allowing them freedom to satisfy their youthful lusts."

"Lusts, is it?" said Mary. "Are you now saying the pair have bedded together?"

"No, no, of course not. It was a poor choice of words. You can have no idea about the urges of a young male; why he'd likely fall in love with any young woman who came his way. He'll soon recover from this fantasy."

"And while he does, he'll not be eager for marriage with me."

"Yes, he will. His father and yours are determined on this match."

"Is not consent supposed to be a part of marriage?" she said. "I'll not consent, no matter what you do."

She turned back toward the house, wanting nothing more than to take her anger out on some inanimate object, to throw something, smash it to pieces as she wanted to smash her father and Harry Percy. But her father's voice stopped her.

"The King has commanded this marriage," he said. "It would not be wise of defy him."

She spun around, stared at her father as though frozen in time.

"So it is true, then," she said. "Lord Percy was refused his bride because the King has his eye on her."

"I cannot answer that," he said.

"Cannot? Or will not?"

"Cannot," said the Earl. "I have no idea why the King is so interested in this match, but it is likely to his advantage. Everything he does is to his advantage."

Mary was still angry, but part of her pitied this Anne Boleyn. Perhaps she did love Lord Percy, but she could never be with the man she loved because the King, a married man, wanted to play with her for a month or two, then toss her aside as he had her sister.

And because of that, she, Mary, would never have the life she wanted, with a husband who could care for her.

***

It was a small church, a village church unaccustomed to accommodate such a large congregation, but it was the best way to do things considering the urgency. The King wanted no public ceremony that would take months to organise; he wanted the marriage done and settled quickly to show all the parties concerned that any future between Percy and Anne Boleyn would never happen.

Harry stood waiting for his bride, his eyes firmly fixed on the altar and the statues behind it. He felt like crying, but as a man he could not do that; all he could do was wish that the woman walking toward him now could be Anne. He even glanced behind him and tried to see Anne there, but his imagination would not rise to such a challenge. It was not Anne, it would never be Anne and he would never see her again.

He had to forget her; that's what his father had told him. Forget her and concentrate on his marriage. As if he could ever forget Anne; even if he lived forever, he could never forget Anne. He was sure his life would run parallel with hers, no matter where either of them found themselves. He would keep a careful watch on where she was and what she was doing, who she was with and more than anything, if she was happy. Her happiness still meant more to him than his own, but he doubted she could be happy in some Irish wasteland with the grave and pious James Butler.

He hoped Anne understood why he was doing this. He had promised her they would be together, even if no consent was forthcoming, and his father had assured him that he would name one of his brothers as his sole heir if he refused to marry Mary. Harry hoped she knew the truth, that he was not afraid of disinheritance, but he was very much afraid of the King's displeasure.

Harry had heard a whisper that it was the King himself who wanted her and if that were true, he was heartbroken to know that his beautiful Anne was being torn away from him and given to that overbearing, over-decorated bully known as the King of England. And it would not last long either; he would soon grow tired of her and cast her aside, as he had others before her. She was worth more than that, much more and Harry would have waited.

He had received a letter from Anne, just this week, in which she assured him that she would never be the King's mistress, even if she had to remain a maid forever. He clung to that, hoped it was because of him. But he did her a disservice; she had assured him in the past, when they were making their plans, that she would go to her husband a true maid.

Harry did not turn to see his bride as she made her slow and reluctant way toward him. If he had, he would have seen that her veil adhered to her face with the tears she shed. He could not know how she dreaded this marriage as much as he did himself.

He only knew what he was told, that Mary Talbot wanted the marriage still, despite knowing the reason for the sudden change in arrangements, and for that he despised her.

They stood in silence as the lengthy ceremony went on for most of the morning, but she did not take his arm as they left the church, husband and wife. Neither felt in the mood for the festivities that followed, when they sat together at the high table, ate as much as their gloomy moods would allow and avoided each other's eyes.

They danced only the formal dances, the ones where they were not required to touch. It was impossible not to think about the night to come. The guests would not ignore it either, as when the minstrels had packed up their instruments ready to leave, the crowd gathered around the newly weds and pulled them from their seats, hurried them to the stairs and up to their bedchamber.

Not one of them noticed how grim the couple looked, how they did not seem happy with the celebrations, how they did not join in the laughter and the gaiety. They were all too intensely enjoying the putting to bed of the newly married couple and, once that was done and the priest had blessed the marriage bed, they all left them alone, in the silence, in the darkness, to stare at the carved ceiling and wish they were anywhere but here.

"They said you wanted our marriage," Mary said. "They told me you had changed your mind about Mistress Boleyn. They lied, did they not?"

"Yes, they lied. I love her and I always will. You should have known that when you insisted we go on with the wedding."

She sat up, glared down at him angrily.

"I insisted?" she cried. "I did not want this. Do you think I want to be tied to a man who loves another woman?"

"So they lied to me, too," said Harry.

"They did."

"It matters not at all. I cannot help but resent the one who took her place."

Mary lay back down, but made no reply. What reply was there to give, after all? It was hardly her fault he could not have his Boleyn slut.

"A fine start to a marriage," she said.

The words were spoken through repressed tears that gathered in her throat.

"We will have to consummate this farce," said Harry. "They will inspect the bedsheets in the morning. If they find no evidence, they'll never let it go."

Mary said nothing for a few moments. He was right; she knew he was right but this was not the way she had imagined giving up her maidenhead. She always hoped it might be with desire, if not love. There was no tenderness in her new husband, no ardour for her as a woman. He hated this as much as she did and she knew in her heart that the only way he would be able to perform this last part of the marriage, was to close his eyes and think of Anne Boleyn.

She pushed back the covers and raised her knees, dropped them to the sides.

"Get it over with quickly, please," she said.

CHAPTER FOUR
The King Commands It!

News that Harry Percy had married reached Anne from the lips of her mother, Elizabeth. Until that moment, she still hoped, still prayed that things would develop as they both wanted, but now that hope died. He was lost to her forever and she felt a numbness spread over her, a sense that nothing mattered any more, nor ever would.

If she only but knew it, many miles away Mary Talbot, now Mary Percy, was feeling the exact same numbness, the same despair and despondency.

Weeks after her return to Hever and the news of Harry's marriage, Anne still felt that despair and she could feel nothing else when she received the news that she was to return to court.

"I have no wish to return to court."

"You do not mean that," said her mother.

"Do not tell me what I mean," said Anne. "Would you want to return to a place where the love of your life has been humiliated before his peers, where everyone knows your business, knows you have been sent away?" She turned to stare out of the window at the fountain below.

"There is nothing for me at court. I cannot smile and pretend all is well, when I know it will never be well again. You may as well proceed with organising my marriage to Mr Butler, send me off to Ireland. I shall feel no different there as here."

"Your marriage to James Butler has been cancelled," said her mother.

She faced her mother with wide and startled eyes. This was something she had not anticipated.

"Why?" she asked.

"The King has decided to cancel it. It is he who commands you to return to court."

"The King commands it?" said Anne.

Her mother smiled knowingly, gave her a sideways glance.

"He has expressed a special interest in you. You should be honoured."

"Like my sister, you mean? As she was honoured?"

Elizabeth pulled herself up stiffly, her mouth turned down with displeasure.

"I only know he has sent for you and that you must return to court. You are to serve Queen Katherine as one of her maids of honour, as you did before. An honour indeed, considering how you disgraced yourself with Lord Percy. Now, please arrange for your boxes to be packed."

Anne knew now what she had not known before, that maid of honour to the Queen was the first step to the King's bed. Well she would have none of it.

The King had his eye on her. Other women might be flattered, but not Anne. She had seen her sister used for his personal pleasure then discarded, she had seen how rich Mary's husband had grown because of it. Anne had no intention of going the same way.

These last months she had dreamed of bedding with Harry Percy, of sharing his love in that intimate way which only people in love should share. To think of sharing that with any other man made her stomach heave and her nerves cringe.

She had heard that King Henry was a handsome man, but she had seen him up close and she did not agree. Once, perhaps, but no more. He was not ugly, to be sure, but handsome was not a word she would have used to describe him.

He was heavy set, not slim and muscular like Harry, and he was several years older than her, not young like Harry. She did not love him and she would never bed with a man she did not love, even if he was the most powerful man in the realm.

She watched her mother go, then picked up the nearest heavy ornament and flung it with full force at the door. The action soothed her temper for but a few minutes before she stood rigidly and contemplated the reality of this news.

"Damn him!" she screamed. "Damn him to hell!"

She failed to notice that one of the maidservants had entered the chamber and was packing her clothes. The woman shrieked and jumped, stared at her mistress and curtsied quickly, terrified that it was she who had caused this bout of temper.

Anne waved her hand to indicate that she should carry on, then turned back to stare once more at the grounds. She welcomed that numbness when it returned but deep down, she knew she would never forgive the King for ruining her life, her dreams of love, only because he had taken a fancy to her himself. She would never forgive the Cardinal for his part in the scheme, nor for upbraiding Harry before his entire household.

These two men would always be her enemy and nothing would ever change that.

***

Anne being received back as a maid of honour to the Queen brought a smile to the face of Sir Thomas Boleyn, if not to his daughter. This was honour indeed; the Boleyn family were moving up in the world at last. Pity his other daughter, Mary, had asked for nothing during her association with the King. Even when she fell pregnant, she asked for nothing, was content to declare the child that of her husband. Of course it could have been, but who will ever know?

He expected more from his other daughter. Anne's present stubbornness was caused only by her disappointment at not being allowed her own choice. She would soon recover from that, soon realise how high she and her family could ascend. It would all work out exactly as Sir Thomas wanted; all he needed to do was give Anne a few days in which to settle then he would instruct her on the ways to the King's heart and, more importantly, to his coffers.

But Anne still found the Queen's household to be tedious and dour. The ladies mostly sat about embroidering or playing the lute and virginals, when they were not praying. That went on several times a day, after the mass that took place every morning, and it was a Catholic mass, something Anne had begun to question. And being there was a bitter reminder of how she had courted Harry Percy. She could not help but seek him out in the evenings, even knowing he would not appear.

She still felt pity for Katherine. She would wait hopefully for her husband to visit her bedchamber at night, but he never did. Once he did come, but deliberately at a time when he must have known she would be at her prayers.

Such behaviour only served to make Anne dislike him even more. If it were true that he had a fancy for her, he would certainly have to change his mind, king or no king.

It was a few weeks after her return to the Queen's household that she was given first hand proof of the King's intentions when he deigned to dance with her. She accepted, of course; she could hardly refuse, but she spoke as little as possible.

"I suspect, Mistress Anne," he said, "that your silence is caused by my presence. I have heard you have much to say to others."

How arrogant!

She turned her dark eyes on him as the dance ended, as the music stopped and she failed to curtsy. Let him make what he would of that.

"I have little to say to the man who has ruined my life, Sire," she said quietly.

His expression showed his shock and anger at such words. Nobody had ever before challenged him in such a way; no one had ever dared. He took her hand and walked from the hall with her, dragging her along as she struggled to keep up with his long strides.

In a smaller chamber, alone, he flung her in front of him and released her abruptly, so abruptly that she almost fell, had to clutch at a chair to keep herself upright. If that was meant to intimidate her, it failed miserably, for such treatment only caused her temper to rise.

"How, pray, have I ruined your life?" he demanded. "I have favoured you with an important position in the Queen's household. How is that ruining your life?"

"You know very well, Your Grace," she said. "I am told it was at the King's pleasure that my betrothal to Harry Percy was denied."

His small eyes scrutinised her, stared her down until she dropped her gaze. It was only then that she realised she should not have spoken to him like that, that he was the King, not just any man. He had power over life and death. Her heart raced as she wondered what punishment he would mete out to her.

"Percy was already promised elsewhere," he said. "His father would never have allowed such a match and besides, he was not good enough for you."

She raised her eyes to stare at him once more, surprised that he would try to excuse his actions to her, when in reality he needed no excuse. His word was law.

"Not good enough?" she replied. "I loved him; he loved me. That was all that was needed."

"Love? You know nothing of love."

He took a step toward her and caught her arms, looked into her face. She wanted to move backward, but there was nowhere to go as the table was behind her.

"I can show you what love really means," he said.

So this was it, this was how it began. It must have been like this for her sister and for Lady Elizabeth Blount, his famous mistress who had served him well, borne him a son and been sent to live out her life in a convent for her troubles. Well, it would not be the same for Anne and he needed to know that.

"Your Grace," she said. "I feel I might have misled you."

He gave a half smile but said nothing, only pulled her just a little closer. He was so tall, Anne's head barely came to his chest and his grip was powerful. She knew full well he could have his way with her if he so wished and she would have nothing to say about it. But that was not King Henry's way; he liked to assure himself that the women he bedded were all madly in love with him. If they were, it would be their loss for Anne had noticed how, when he had tired of them, they were discarded and forgotten, left to their own fate like poor Bessie Blount whose husband refused to take her back. At least Mary Boleyn had a husband to fall back on, whereas Lady Blount's husband wanted none of her.

Even the Queen had been ignored by this King for months, for no better reason than that she had grown old and could not longer conceive. He saw as little of her in private as he could manage.

"How so?" he asked at last. "How have you misled me?"

"I am accustomed to the French court," she said. "Things are a different there, a little more flirtatious and gay. An Englishman might consider a certain look to be an invitation, when it is no such thing."

He frowned. This was new to him; when he set his sights on a woman, she was usually anxious to please, if only for the favours with which she would be rewarded. Indeed, the sister had been willing enough, too willing if truth be told. He expected this Boleyn girl to be of a similar nature.

He pulled her tighter into his arms then, held her close to his chest and listened to her racing heart. That assured him that her words were only empty ones.

"Anne," he said, in a tone he thought seductive. "My heart leapt when first I laid eyes on you. I have tried to resist my own emotions, but I find myself in love with you. Your every look, your every gesture brings me joy."

She tried to move away from him, but he was too strong. She had no choice other than to talk against his massive chest.

"I am sorry to hear that, Sire," she said.

"Sorry? Why should you be sorry?"

"Because you are a married man, Your Grace, and should be making such advances only to your wife."

He pushed her away then, caught her just before she hit the table behind, then stood her on her feet.

"You dare to speak to me like that?"

Her lip trembled and she wondered briefly if this night she would spend in the Tower. But she had no intention of becoming his mistress and he needed to know that, the sooner the better.

"I meant no disrespect, Your Grace," she said. "I wished only to set your mind at rest."

"Set my mind at rest?" he said, his voice rising. "You have torn my heart to shreds with your words." He paused, moved away from her.

"But perhaps you misunderstand my meaning," he said.

"It is possible, Sire," she said.

"Then let me make it clear. I long for you, Anne. I yearn for your pretty little duckies to be close to me in bed. I love you and I want you. Can I make it any clearer?"

"You cannot, Your Grace," she replied. "You want me for your mistress."

He smiled.

"I do. May I come to your bedchamber tonight?"

"No."

"No? You suggest we meet somewhere else?"

"No, that is not what I am saying, Sire."

"What then? I will meet you anywhere you wish, I will give you anything you wish. Tell me, please, put me out of my misery."

"That I cannot do, Sire," she said. "I have promised myself that I will go to my husband a true maid. That is a promise that is precious to me and I will not give it up for any man."

He could not believe it. This slip of a girl, who should be honoured by his attention, was turning him down. How could that be? But she was merely attempting to increase his ardour, that was it.

"You are teasing me, Anne," he said.

"No such thing, Your Grace," she said. "I refuse to be any man's mistress." She curtsied then and went on. "May I return to the dance now, Sire?"

He nodded, not knowing what to say, and she hurried from the room before he changed his mind.

***

That was how it began. At every opportunity, the King pursued Anne, and always she refused him. The whole court was talking about it; indeed, the whole of London were talking about it.

It was unfortunate for Anne that not one of those gossipmongers admired her for standing out against the King, not one of them saw that she was right to refuse to let a married man into her bed, not one of them admired her for wanting to keep herself pure for any future husband. But the way the King was besotted, it seemed unlikely she would ever have such a husband, as he would never consent to her marriage to anyone and no gentleman would dare to ask.

Henry made no secret of his infatuation with Mistress Anne Boleyn, not to his advisors, not to his courtiers and certainly not to his wife. She it was who was compelled to suffer the woman's presence, each and every day in her household.

At first, Katherine not only tolerated Anne, but was particularly friendly to her. She was happy enough to welcome someone her husband was so fond of, if it pleased him, but now she felt she was being made a fool of.

She wanted to dismiss Anne, and Anne would most certainly have not objected, but the King would have none of it.

"Sire," she pleaded with him. "You are making it difficult for me. The Queen casts evil looks my way, the other ladies resent me."

Henry stepped close to her, held her face in his warm hand and smiled.

"Dearest Anne," he said. "That is not my wish. I will speak with the Queen about it."

"No. I do not want you to speak with the Queen about it. I want you to stop pestering me."

"Pestering?" His voice thundered through the empty room as he stepped away from her. "Is that really how you see it? I have pursued you for months because I love you; I cannot stop thinking about you. I dream of you at night, I see you everywhere in the day. And you call it pestering?"

Was this it? Was it the answer to make him so angry he would despise her? She could only hope.

"I know your feelings, Your Grace," she said. "But I do not return them. I wish to be released to find an honourable man who will marry me."

He was silent for a long time, so long that she turned to study his expression. Had she displeased him with her words? Had she angered him enough that he would cast her into the Tower, or leave her alone and find another on whom to settle his affection?

"Marriage?" he demanded. "Is that what you want?"

Oh no! He had taken her words completely the wrong way.

"No," she replied. "At least not marriage with anyone. I loved Harry Percy; I still love him, but you and your priest have made it impossible for me to have him. I can never love any man as I loved him, but I would like to try. I cannot do that while you have this hold over me. Will you give me leave to try? Please."

He shook his head.

"Never. I could never part with you, never think of you with another man. If it is marriage you want, then marriage you shall have."

She caught her breath. Now she was quite certain he had lost his mind.

"You cannot offer me marriage while Katherine lives," she said. "You know it and I know it. The whole world knows it, so why even mention it?"

"I'll find a way, Anne. I swear, I'll find a way."

"There is no way."

She looked at him with fear in her eyes. Henry was a man who had never been refused anything he ever wanted and if he was determined to find a way to annul his marriage to Katherine, he might well succeed. And where would that leave Anne? Compelled to marry a man she resented and had sworn to despise, and one she found unappealing.

CHAPTER FIVE
Poison, That's What!

Four years since her marriage and Mary Percy wished for that numbness to return, to aid her through whatever the future might have to offer.

Harry had consummated their marriage, but since then he kept to his own chamber, until some two months later when he came to hers one night as she had just got into bed. The maidservants had gone, left her alone, and she settled down to sleep, expecting this night to be no different from any other.

That was when he entered, that was when he approached the bed and stood staring down at her. She rolled over onto her back and looked up at him, a little dart of fear making her heart leap as she wondered what he wanted.

He had scarcely spoken to her since the wedding, except to tell her he'd not have Cardinal Wolsey's servants in his house. Just why he told her that, she could not know. Perhaps he believed the attempt to have them here was her idea; who knew?

"You have not conceived?" he said.

"You might have noticed if I had," she replied.

"Then it would be best to make a further attempt," he said. "You can give me nothing that I want, except an heir."

She scrambled to a sitting position, drew her legs up to her chest and clutched the covers.

"No," she said. "Not again."

"You'll do your duty, Madam," he said, "as I must do mine. Do you imagine I want to be here? But you must at least try to give me a son."

Then he pulled the covers out of her clenched fist and climbed into the bed beside her. She slid away from him, tried to get her feet onto the floor, but he grabbed her and flung her back onto the bed. He pushed her shift up and forced himself into her, while she struggled and tried to push him off, but he was too strong.

When he had finished, he rolled away and stood up.

"Damn you!" she cried. "Is it my fault I am not your beloved Anne?"

"If you were Anne, I'd have cherished you."

"And if you were a real man, I might have cherished you."

He slapped her then, leaving an angry mark on her cheek which would turn to a bruise by morning. The sound of her sobbing followed him out of the chamber and filled him with shame.

He lay awake that night for hours, trying to fathom why he had done that, why he had gone to her in the first place, why he had forced himself on her and why he had hit her. It was not in his nature to be violent, but he was still so angry and frustrated with his marriage, still aching about losing Anne. He had to take his fury out on someone, and Mary happened to be available. He despised her, but she did not deserve such treatment.

That night he retired to his bed and thought about his life as it had become, compared it to the life he had wanted with Anne, and his anger had grown like a monster within. He had to have something that would make what remained of his life worthwhile, and he could think of nothing he wanted from his wife but an heir.

Yet he knew in his heart it was no fault of Mary's, that she resented him as much as he resented her. He had a right to use her if he so wished, but that was not how he wanted his marriage to be. And he had no right to hit her; that was unforgiveable.

He came to her the following morning, where she sat at her meal in the great hall. He never broke his fast with her, so she was wary at this sudden courtesy as he slid into a chair across the table from her and waited until the last servant had gone.

"I came to apologise," he said. "I lost my temper last night and I had no right to strike you."

Mary did not expect this and had no idea what to say, so she said nothing. Perhaps that made it worse, she would never know, because he got to his feet after a few minutes and left her alone. Nothing more was said on the subject.

Since then there had been little contact between them and Mary felt that she was living on the edge of a precipice, wondering when he would push her over, make another attempt, wondering when he would lose his temper again.

The surprising thing was not that he resented her, as she resented him, but that Anne Boleyn loved him. How could she? What man did she see in Lord Percy that Mary had never seen? He despised Mary for not being Anne and Mary despised him because he loved Anne. It was a recipe for an unhappy marriage, and that is how it had developed. He would never get over her, that was for certain and Mary wondered if Anne felt the same, now that the King of England was pursuing her. Such exalted company could well push Harry out of her heart, but Mary knew that Anne still wrote to Harry, still wrote fondly.

Now she watched him as he rode away. He had work to do protecting the borders of his county, his slackness in that direction having recently caused the King himself to complain.

Harry was now the Earl of Northumberland, since his father died the year before, and when he thought about Anne, he wished only that the old man could have died earlier, when Harry would have been able to decide for himself who his bride should be.

But of course, that was foolish. The King had his sights set on her so nothing he did or said could have made a difference. And it was so unfair. Anne did not want King Henry; she did not want him then and she did not want him now, but still he pursued her, still he would not allow her the freedom to live the life she had always expected.

The whole country was gossiping about how Anne would not give in to the King's desires. He knew not how she was holding him at bay or how much longer she could do so. Surely he would grow weary of the chase, but it seemed he just grew more determined. It might be better for her if she gave in to him; he might leave her alone then, might decide that the chase was far more pleasurable than the prize.

Mary had been passing his chamber that morning when she noticed that the door was open. She had no real reason to stop, to look inside, but a movement drew her attention and she saw that he was sitting at his desk, the top drawer open. That was a drawer that was usually locked; Mary knew, because she had tried several times to open it.

She moved into the doorway, just far enough to see that her husband held in his hand a miniature portrait of a young woman with dark hair and eyes, a young woman named Anne Boleyn. She caught back a sob, a sound which made him turn to her and jump to his feet.

"So," he said. "You spy on me for yourself as well as for Norfolk."

"What are you talking about?" she answered.

She cursed herself for the sudden and unexpected emotion that escaped her. She had no love for her husband, indeed she despised him with all her strength, but to know that he still hankered after the Boleyn trollop was just too much to stomach.

"I know you have been spying on me and reporting back to Norfolk," he shouted. "How else does the King know my every action?"

"You are wrong," she said. "I have done no such thing."

"I do not believe you."

"I care nothing for your beliefs. I was distressed at seeing you with her portrait, after all this time."

"Why should you care?"

"I do not care about your love for her, but about the disrespect to me."

He tossed the portrait back into the drawer and locked it.

"It is none of your concern," he told her.

"Why do you not give her up?" Mary demanded. "She has ruined your life, and mine and now it seems the King himself is under her spell. She is known as the King's whore."

"And that is a lie," he said. "She has denied him all this time."

"Word is she has denied him to increase his ardour."

"She has denied him in the hope he will give up the pursuit and allow her to leave court."

She scoffed.

"You have word from her?"

He made no reply. She had no need to know about the occasional message he received from Anne, nor did she need to know that he lived for those letters, that the anticipation of them was all he ever looked forward to.

When he left his wife that morning, he failed to notice the almost white colour of her complexion, nor the little beads of perspiration that clung to her forehead. Why should he notice things of that nature, he who had never wanted her, he whom she despised?

But at the end of the day, he arrived back at Alnwick Castle to find maidservants running about Mary's chamber with cold water and cloths, and a physician in attendance.

For one moment his heart leapt with hope as his first thought was that she was dying. Could he be free of her at last? Would he have some peace before his own end came, which he expected to be early since he was often ill, often shaking and sweating himself.

But *he* did not hurry to send for physicians and take to his bed. She was likely but seeking attention after his apology of the morning.

Yet he could be wrong; she could be really ill and if she was, he could be free. He would never remarry; there was still only one woman he wanted in his life and the man who stood in his way was too powerful to challenge. At least he might have some peace in the years that were left to him.

He made his way to his wife's chamber in time to see the physician removing fat little shiny leeches. The man turned to him.

"Ah, My Lord," he said. "I am glad you have returned. Her Ladyship has been very ill today, very ill indeed. I must say I am surprised you noticed nothing this morning."

"What is wrong with her?" he replied abruptly.

"She has a stomach ague, vomiting and loose bowels."

Harry grimaced. He hated talk about bodily ailments.

"What do you think was the cause?" he asked.

"Poison, that's what!" mumbled a weak voice from the bed. "He has poisoned me."

"Hush, My Lady," said the physician. "You do not mean that."

"Do not tell me what I mean." Mary struggled to keep her voice audible. "He's tried to do away with me so he can have his Boleyn whore!"

The physician stepped back from the bed in shock, then turned to Harry.

"I fear Her Ladyship is delirious, My Lord," he said.

Harry only stared back at him angrily. He was furious with Mary for making such accusations, especially before a physician and the servants. He would love to be rid of her, but he was not about to hang for it.

"You may leave now," he said. "And if you breathe a word of my wife's accusation, I will make your life unbearable."

He closed the door on the man and turned to the bed. She did look ill; there was no doubting that. She was very pale; she had that film of stickiness over her skin.

"Do you really believe I would poison you?" he asked her.

"Are you denying it?"

"Of course I am. I do not love you, I would not be sorry to see you go, but you are not worth hanging for."

He left her then, not knowing that she forced herself out of bed, weak though she was, and wrote a pleading letter to her father.

***

Mary's health improved slowly and she was confined to bed for some weeks, but her husband refused to allow the doctors to apply the ghastly little leeches to her body.

No doubt they would all take that to mean he wanted her health to fail, but so be it. They could do whatever else they liked but Harry was convinced she was weaker after the application of the blood sucking little monsters.

Harry looked down at her, where she lay still pale and weak. He would have liked to smile, to reassure her, but he found he could not do that. He hated her too much to offer her any solace.

It was of the utmost importance to Harry that Mary lived; if she should die now, after her accusation, he could find himself on trial for her murder. The state of their marriage was no secret and that would be evidence enough to hang him.

The first of her father's servants arrived before she was fully recovered, carrying a letter from him to Harry, accusing him of abusing his wife and of trying to poison her. He demanded that Harry allow the servants to see Mary, to be sure she was uninjured.

Harry was furious. Abused her? He would never think of such a thing. Once, he had lost his fragile temper and struck her and had immediately regretted it. He had apologised profusely, but he should not be surprised that she was now reporting that one incident to her father.

He refused to allow them access to his wife, sent them away without a reply for Lord Shrewsbury.

He would like to have excluded her servants, but she needed help with everything until she recovered. Harry could find no sympathy for her, no compassion. He knew the servants were giving her news of the latest gossip, but he could not care any more.

He visited her to see if she was recovering, to be sure he was right about the leeches. A maidservant was just leaving and gave him a quick curtsy, her eyes showing fear as she hurried past him.

Mary was dressed for the first time in weeks, but her clothes hung on her as she had lost so much weight.

She was unable to stand for long and after a few minutes, sank into the chair beside the window. She looked up at him defiantly.

"You refused to allow the physicians to treat me," she said accusingly. "Did you hope to speed my death?"

"I refused because I thought you too weak to take more blood letting."

"You mean you did it for my sake?"

"Partly, but mostly I did it for mine. I did not want you to die after accusing me of trying to kill you." He paused and moved to sit in the chair beside her. "It seems I was right. You are able to leave your bed, although you still do not seem well. Perhaps a taste of fresh air might aid you."

"It might." Mary wondered if she should mention the gossip she had just that minute heard from the servant, but she decided to find out for certain if it were true. "I hear congratulations are in order, My Lord," she said.

He gave her a puzzled frown.

"How so?"

"I was told your whore had given you a daughter," she said. "Isabel, is it not?"

He made no reply. He had hoped to keep the child a secret as well as his relationship with her mother, but it mattered not at all. It was not as though he loved the woman; he would never love anyone but Anne, but he would willingly support his daughter.

"I am entitled to comfort from someone," he replied. "Yes, I have a daughter and I shall support her, and I am fond of her mother, but I do not love her."

"Of course not. You still love the Boleyn trollop."

"I know not why you must call her that. She is no such thing, as you well know, and I cannot believe it is jealousy that fuels your words."

"No, certainly not jealousy," said Mary. "How would you feel if you were forced to marry a woman you knew was in love with someone else?"

"I would likely feel the same," he said. "It would certainly cause an unhappy marriage."

"Well then, why should I not resent the bitch?"

Harry felt his fingers twitching with the need to strike out and he wondered if he would ever feel less defensive of Anne. He knew this conversation was going nowhere. How could it, when there was no solution to their problems? Before he could change the subject, a servant appeared to announce the arrival of the Duke of Norfolk.

"Well, we are honoured to have such an exalted visitor," said Harry sarcastically.

Mary looked up hopefully. Norfolk was her ally and he knew it, but she wondered if she would be permitted to see him or if Harry would send him away as he had her father's servants.

The Duke waited in the great hall, seated in the most comfortable armchair as though he were the master of the house, but he got to his feet when Harry appeared.

"Your Grace," Harry said at once. "I am honoured by your visit, but also puzzled. You seem to know everything I am doing by means of my wife. What else is there to know?"

"You are wrong, My Lord," he said. "But no matter. I came not to discover your movements but to relay my concerns, and Lord Shrewsbury's concerns, about the way you have been treating your wife."

"Really, Your Grace? And what business is that of yours?"

"I was asked to come here, to tell you it has gone on long enough. You must change your ways, you must treat Lady Mary with affection and respect. She has done her best to be a good wife to you."

"Is that what she told you? Well, I beg to differ, but that is neither here nor there. The fact of the matter is, her father forced this marriage on her, even whilst knowing that I loved another woman. He can hardly complain now that the marriage is unsuccessful. What else would he expect?"

"You could never have had Anne Boleyn. That is obvious now."

"It is, but it was not obvious then and I did love her. I still do."

"That is dangerous talk, My Lord."

"Perhaps." Harry paused and looked at the Duke thoughtfully. "What do you want me to do? I cannot love Mary; I cannot even like her."

"But you must. You have sworn to it."

Suddenly it was all too much. He deeply resented the intrusion into his private affairs and he knew well that both he and Mary would be happier apart.

"I'll tell you what you must do," he said at last. "You must take her with you. Return her to her father. I should be happy never to see her again as long as I live."

He turned then, left the Duke open jawed and went upstairs to Mary's bedchamber, where she still waited to see if he was going to give the Duke access to her. He sat in the chair beside her.

"What have you been telling your father?" he said. "First he sends his servants with letters accusing me of beating you, and I know you told him I tried to poison you. Now he sends his ally to tell me how to behave."

"You did hit me," she answered.

"Once, years ago." He got to his feet and turned to look down at her. "Norfolk is downstairs, waiting to take you with him and return you to your father. Are you well enough to travel?"

"What are you saying?"

"I think it would be the best thing for us both if we parted. Do you not concede?"

"Well," she said. "It seems we have finally found something on which we can agree."

"I will be happy if I never see you again and I am sure you feel the same."

CHAPTER SIX
A Royal Bastard

Anne was recovering from sweating sickness, which had taken her away from court at last. She had never been so ill in her life and even there, Henry would not leave her in peace to rest. He had to write several times a week, had to send his emissaries to see how she fared, and at times she wished herself dead.

Nobody knew that she still corresponded with Harry Percy and if the King found out, it would likely be the end of Harry. She hoped that this time away from Henry might make him realise he could do without her, that he need not alienate the country by divorcing his lawful Queen. She wondered, too, if the country would ever forgive her for being the focus of their King's ardour, for being his obsession. The lies that were told about her distressed her terribly, but she could do nothing to challenge them.

People said she was scheming to get her hands on the crown. It was rumoured that she denied the King, refused to satisfy his lust in order to increase his desire, but that was not it, not at all.

The fact was she did not want him, had never wanted him. She found him unattractive, but although she had told him many truths that no other would have dared to tell him, that was one truth too far. Even she dared not tell him that he was not the handsome young man he had been when he succeeded to the throne.

Now she was forced to serve the Queen who hated her and Princess Mary who also hated her. But it had lasted for years and she could not persuade the King that she would be happier if he allowed her to marry and have a normal life.

When she told him she would go chastely to her husband, that she would not give herself to any man outside of marriage, he had assumed she wanted marriage to him. He was so vain, he believed every woman he met fell instantly in love with him. He could never imagine that most of them complied because he was the King and they were afraid to refuse him. Anne was the first one he had met who was not afraid, and not scared to voice her thoughts.

But now she was recovering from her illness and the King wanted her back at court. It seemed there was no escape.

Her latest letter from Harry told her that he and his wife had parted, never to see each again and that made her sad. She had wanted nothing but happiness for Harry, even though she longed for him with every waking thought, and it grieved her that his marriage was unhappy and that she was the cause.

Now the King had taken an unbelievable step; he had started proceedings to divorce Queen Katherine. Anne could hold him at bay no longer; she had tried to tell him she did not want him, but the words never would come out as intended. Always there was the ultimate excuse, that he was a married man and she, Anne, would not give herself outside of marriage, especially not to a married man.

She would have to return to court, she would have to persuade him, but to tell him the truth would be a death sentence. Either that, or he would refuse to believe her.

It seemed to Anne that she was trapped and there was no way out. Harry belonged to another, and now it was dangerous for her to keep up their correspondence. She had to write that last letter, had to tell him she could write no more.

And she would have to comply with the King's wishes. She did not want to give in to him, to let him have his way with her and perhaps get her with child and discard her like the others. And then, if he released her and allowed her to marry someone, she would not be able to go to her husband a virgin, and that was something that was very important to her.

There was only one thing to do. She would have to pretend to want this as much as he did and hope that divorcing Katherine proved to be the impossibility she hoped it would.

***

Mary had gone and the castle seemed strangely empty without her. Not that Harry missed her in the way that he still missed Anne, but he had not yet had time to grow accustomed to not having to worry about her sudden appearance, about the resentment that appearance brought to him. The glares across the table at dinner, the concern that he would never have an heir to the Northumberland title and estates. He was on bad terms with both his brothers and would be sure to avoid leaving the title to either one of them.

He also never appreciated how much Mary did until servants came to him with questions and requests for instructions that should come from the Countess. Harry would never have thought that sending Mary away would double his workload, but at least she would not be spying on him any more.

That was when he received the letter. His heart sang as it always did when he saw her seal and he ripped it open, longing to just read her words, even though they had nothing new to impart. But she would write that she loved him still, that she hoped one day the King would grow tired and he might be able to free himself from Mary through an annulment.

But they were all empty dreams and deep down they both knew it. This letter killed those dreams, this letter told him firmly that he had been fooling himself all these years.

She said she would not be able to write to him again. She told him of the King's plans to divorce the Queen and marry her and that it would be too dangerous for them both to keep up their correspondence.

That correspondence was all he had left of the love of his life and she was telling him he was about to lose it. Harry felt like crying.

***

Back at court, Anne felt herself out of place. Things had changed since her illness, people looked at her differently and a few people asked her to intervene with the King on various matters. That was new and not something in which she wanted to involve herself. She still hoped to be free of him, not immerse herself even more in his affections. She would ask for nothing, so he would have nothing with which to reproach her when the time came.

But back in the Queen's household, several of the other maids of honour gave her evil looks and the Queen herself glared at her. She asked nothing of her so that Anne felt no more real than one of the statues about the place.

Henry came to her apartment at the first opportunity, his smile one of delight to have her back and fully recovered. He held out his arms to her, but she did not move into them. He seemed not to notice as he pulled her toward him and kissed her. Neither did he notice the grimace as she smelled his breath.

"Sweetheart," he said. "I have missed you so. And I need your counsel. I have finally realised what God has been telling me all this time."

"And what is that, Your Grace?"

"That my marriage to Katherine was never a true one, never lawful. She was my brother's widow and marrying her was against God's law; it says so clearly enough in the Bible."

"The Bible has not changed, has it?" she said bitterly. "It had the same rule then, when you married Katherine?"

"It did and the Pope should never have given me a dispensation to marry her. It was his fault."

Of course, it would be anyone's fault but not his, not Henry's.

"But he did give that dispensation. Therefore, your marriage was lawful."

"Do you not see, sweetheart?" he insisted. "It is the reason I have one useless girl and nothing but dead boys. God is telling me it is because I went against Him, because I defied His law."

"Henry, think carefully about this. You are like a child who has never been refused anything and now, because you have found something you cannot have, you must have it no matter what."

He stepped back, pushed her roughly away.

"How dare you! You speak to your King that way?"

"Did you not tell me once that when you are with me you are not a King, but a man like any other?"

"I did, but still it was a cruel thing to say."

"It was the truth."

He slowly shook his head, turned away and was silent for a few minutes. Then he turned back to her, his smile in place once more.

"I know what you are doing, Anne," he said. "You are so warm and caring, you are trying to protect Katherine. Is that not it?"

"Protect Katherine? Yes, I would like to protect Katherine. She has been a good and faithful wife to you and now you would discard her when she is inconvenient. How do I know you'll not do the same to me?"

"It is different with you. I never loved Katherine."

"You did."

"Not as I love you. I would never betray you."

"You will do as you wish, Sire," she said. "I can say nothing that will dissuade you."

He failed to notice the defeat in her voice.

***

So it began. Cardinal Wolsey assembled a jury of churchmen and nobles to try the case of the King's marriage, whether it be lawful, and Henry hoped for a speedy outcome in his favour.

He declared before the court that his marriage was an abomination, against God's law, that the Almighty was telling him clearly His will, by denying him healthy sons.

Anne knew that was untrue, that had Katherine given him an heir he would never have considered such a thing, and she listened intently, praying the eminent jurors would not be fooled by such a plea. But it seemed to her that everyone was listening too intently.

Anne listened, hidden in an alcove, and smiled. This man who had pursued her, this man who would cause a scandal throughout Christendom and risk his own soul for her, could persuade himself that black was white if such was to his advantage.

After weeks of deliberation, the court decided they could give no verdict and Cardinal Wolsey declared it was beyond his learning to give one either. He would send to Rome for instructions; the Pope must decide.

Henry was enraged. He came to Anne's apartment, poured himself wine and turned to her while she hid her face, hoping he would not notice her complacency.

"I am the King of England!" he shouted. "When I pray, God answers and He has told me what I must do. How dare they think the Pope's word takes precedence over God's!"

"But Henry, the Pope is the head of the Church. He must decide what is right, surely. He is the authority on God's law."

"God is the authority on God's law." He sat beside her, took her hand. "Forgive me, Anne. I know this is as hard for you as it is for me."

No! No it is not hard for me!

"Henry," she said soothingly, "perhaps this outcome is God's way of telling you our love is not to be."

"What are you saying?" He caught her in his arms and kissed her passionately. "We will be together! I have sworn to make you my queen and I shall keep that promise. To hell with the Pope. Who is he to tell the King of England what to do?"

She pulled his head to her and stroked his hair, sighed resignedly. She knew then, knew that he would have his own way eventually, no matter how long it took, no matter how many lives he trampled on to get there.

And once he had achieved his goal, what would become of that goal? What would become of Anne?

***

The papal legate came at last, after months of waiting, to begin a new trial to decide whether King Henry's marriage to Queen Katherine was lawful or not.

Cardinal Campeggio arrived in London just before Yuletide, sent by the Pope at the request of Cardinal Wolsey, who had been unable to try the case himself.

The Italian Cardinal was ancient and the long journey had been a deterrent to his health. The court could not sit until after the Christmas festivities and holy days, then the Cardinal was sent to Katherine, to advise her that her best option would be to retreat to a convent.

He was shocked when she refused.

"I am a married woman," she protested. "I will remain a married woman."

Then she produced the dispensation given by Pope Julius II which allowed her marriage to take place. She had sworn before God that her marriage to Prince Arthur, Henry's brother, had not been consummated and that had suited Henry at the time. Now he wanted to be rid of her, he produced witnesses to remember Arthur's boasting, the morning after his wedding night, when he declared himself thirsty because he had spent the night 'deep inside Spain'.

Arthur was fifteen and embarrassed that he had been unable to perform his marital duty, but rather than admit that, he boasted of the opposite.

This bragging was also dismissed as such when Henry wanted to marry his widow; now he wanted rid of her, so that he could marry Anne, he decided to believe his late brother's words.

It was June before the trial began, as Cardinal Campeggio delayed at every turn and when the King discovered that he did not have the full authority of the Pope after all, he was infuriated.

The atmosphere inside the court was filled with tension and gloom. The parties involved showed little emotion, but it was apparent that they were both tense and for different reasons.

Henry wanted only to obtain his divorce, to be told that he was right, God was telling him he had committed a terrible sin by marrying his brother's widow. But all the time he knew well his real reasons for wanting to be rid of Katherine; he wanted Anne Boleyn and she would accept nothing less than marriage. He also wanted a son, which Katherine could no longer give him. Which of these was the more important to Henry, it was difficult to tell, but it was a fact that the Tudor dynasty was too new to survive without a direct heir to the throne.

If anyone doubted that Henry's stated reason for this hearing, at the specially convened Legatine court at Blackfriars, was genuine, they would never voice their doubts. What they did know was that the outcome of this hearing could change their own lives forever, for if a King could discard a faithful and blameless Queen, a princess of Spain, it set a precedent for the future of the crown.

What they did not know was that the Pope had received, anonymously, letters written by King Henry to Mistress Anne Boleyn. They gave the lie to the pretence that his need for an annulment was God's will. The Cardinal from Rome had no idea who had sent them, but he intended to keep the knowledge of them to himself.

Henry addressed the court, first declaring his love for Katherine and his sorrow at having to take this step, but take it he must, for he had disobeyed God's law by marrying her and he had been punished for that disobedience by the birth of dead and dying sons.

Next, Katherine was called upon to give her statement and, instead of standing and stating her case, she walk rapidly to where the King sat and sank down onto her knees on the stone floor.

"Sir, I beseech you for all the love that has been between us, and for the love of God, let me have justice. Take of me some pity and compassion, for I am a poor woman, and a stranger born out of your dominion. I have here no assured friends, and much less impartial counsel...

"Alas! Sir, wherein have I offended you, or what occasion of displeasure have I deserved? I have been to you a true, humble and obedient wife, ever comfortable to your will and pleasure, that never said or did anything to the contrary thereof, being always well pleased and contented with all things wherein you had any delight or dalliance, whether it were in little or much. I never grudged in word or countenance, or showed a visage or spark of discontent. I loved all those whom you loved, only for your sake, whether I had cause or no, and whether they were my friends or enemies. This twenty years or more I have been your true wife and by me you have had many children, although it has pleased God to call them out of this world, which has been no fault of mine.

"When you had me at first, I take God to my judge, I was a true maid, without touch of man. And whether it be true or no, I put it to your conscience. If there be any just cause by the law that you can allege against me either of dishonesty or any other impediment to banish and put me from you, I am well content to depart to my great shame and dishonour. And if there be none, then here, I most lowly beseech you, let me remain in my former estate. Therefore, I most humbly require you, in the way of charity and for the love of God – who is the just judge – to spare me the extremity of this new court, until I may be advised what way and order my friends in Spain will advise me to take. And if ye will not extend to me so much impartial favour, your pleasure then be fulfilled, and to God I commit my cause!"

While she spoke, Henry tried on several occasions to lift her to her feet, but she resisted with all her strength and stayed on her knees.

But when she had said her piece, she got up and walked out of court, ignoring every summons to return.

"It is no impartial court for me, therefore I will not tarry. Go on," she ordered those who called her back. "I commend my case to God."

The King was enraged, not only because of Katherine's words, but because she had mentioned her friends in Spain, as though they had any authority over the law of England.

Henry was questioned as to the Queen's plea and he agreed with everything she had said, but he insisted that it was his conscience and God's will that brought him here. He told them all that were it not for that, he would never want to part from Katherine, whom he loved dearly.

Anne listened to the proceedings, hidden behind a curtain, and she smiled. Her admiration for Katherine had always been great, but now it soared. The Queen left her husband, the King, bewildered and enraged, as he had no means to recall her. He had been made a fool of and he would have his revenge.

Anne prayed that this would be the end of it, that he would now give up the fight and allow her to leave. Her prayers went unanswered.

Henry allowed himself a few days to control his temper before he visited Katherine. Her ladies dropped into deep curtsies when he appeared; it had been a very long time since he had been seen in his wife's chambers.

His eyes lingered on Anne, but he made no indication that there was anything more intimate between them. He liked to tell himself it was a secret, although the whole country knew of his wishes for her.

He waved his hand to dismiss them all, then turned to Katherine, who had knelt when he entered and now stayed on her knees. He stepped forward, took her arms and lifted her gently to her feet.

"Henry," she said, catching his hand and kissing it. "You are here as my husband?"

"No, My Lady," he replied harshly. "I am here as your King. Your recent display has done you no favours, only made me more convinced of the sinfulness of our union." He paused, pulled his hand away from her. "Do you not see that I am right? How else can you explain your failure to provide an heir?"

Katherine could think of many reasons why God might be angry with them, not least of which was Henry's infidelity and Katherine's acceptance of that infidelity. There was also his insistence that every thought that entered his kingly head, had to come directly from God himself. But she voiced none of those.

"I am but a feeble woman," she said. "I have given you my love; is it my fault that God has taken my sons?"

"Yes, Katherine, it is your fault," he replied. "It is both our faults. We must separate; our marriage was never lawful."

"It was lawful and you know it."

"No, I do not. This court is taking too long and all that time is wasted, when we could be putting our lives in order to please God. I want you to agree to an annulment."

"And make our daughter a bastard?"

"If you do not do as I say, you will never see your daughter again," said Henry. "I shall make sure of that."

He left her then, left her astonished and hurt that this man, whom she had loved for most of her life, would keep her apart from the only person left to her to love.

With an ache in her heart, she remembered those twenty years of happy marriage, those nights when he had come to her bedchamber and loved her, held her close in his arms and kissed her lips. And it was not only for the making of a son; it was with real love that he did those things, but it was pointless to torture herself with those memories. Now she had to be strong and determined, for the sake of her daughter.

She could scarce believe he would do that to Mary, make her a bastard, deprive her of her place in the line of succession to the throne. But that was what he was doing, by trying to establish that their marriage was unlawful. He had made much of Mary; he had made her Princess of Wales in her own right, something that had never been done before, he had sought for her a betrothal to the finest princes in Europe, and now he would declare her a bastard, a nothing, no better than Bessie Blount's son, worse even, since he was a boy and Henry had given him a grand title.

Katherine would not give in to his demands. She knew the truth and it had nothing to do with his conscience; she and Mary were to suffer to satisfy the King's lust. She was a daughter of Ferdinand and Isabella, those great Catholic princes, and she would not allow it. She would fight him with her last breath, but deep down she could not believe that he meant what he said. She was wrong.

The following day, the King ordered that Katherine be removed from court. She was no longer the Queen, he said. She was the Dowager Princess of Wales, widow of Prince Arthur Tudor, and her child, Mary, was a bastard.

The suitors who had pursued Princess Mary's hand in marriage fell away, as they had no wish to be married to a royal bastard.

CHAPTER SEVEN
Mary Percy's Request

Although she had never met her or even seen her in the flesh, Mary Percy often wondered, as she settled into her old chambers at her father's house, just what it was about Anne Boleyn that attracted both her husband and the King. Mary had seen her portrait and thought her a plain looking young woman with a double chin, which she tried to hide with her bands of velvet and her high necklaces.

Knowing this made Mary smile. She had no flaws she had to hide with clothes or jewellery, yet there was something about Anne. She had courtiers following her everywhere and she had been alone in keeping the King at arm's length for all these years. No other woman had ever achieved that, or perhaps no other woman had tried.

People said that she did it to increase his interest, that she was determined to oust Katherine and take her place as Queen. Indeed, the King had started divorce proceedings, although they had not gone to plan. Mary heard from her friend, Lucinda Hampton, that Anne had been heard to say she hoped the divorce never happened and that Henry would leave her alone.

Mary did not believe it. She did not pretend to know the woman who had ruined her marriage and her future, the woman her husband adored, but she did not see her as an innocent. In her eyes, Anne was a scheming witch, intent on the throne.

Mary resented being here, in her father's house. She was the Countess of Northumberland and should be at Alnwick Castle, residing over it as its mistress. Instead she was here, under the rule of her father where no married woman should be.

And her father refused to take any of the blame for the situation. As far as he was concerned, the entire fault lay with Harry Percy, the Earl of Northumberland. He was still convinced the man was unreasonable, that he had tried to poison his daughter and that he had abused her. The failure of the marriage was Percy's fault, and his alone.

Mary told her father when she first arrived that he was the one to blame, that he should never have forced the marriage on them, knowing Harry loved someone else, knowing he had no wish to marry Mary.

"But I did not realise then, my dear, what an unreasonable man he was," said her father.

"Any normal man would have been enchanted with you, would have soon forgotten his infatuation. But no, he had to keep up this stubborn insistence on a fantasy, he would not give any effort to building a marriage with you."

He was right, of course, but she would not tell him so. He should never have forced the marriage, neither should the old Earl of Northumberland, but both thought they knew best, both believed that once wed, everything else would be buried in the past.

Then there was the King; he, too, had a part in ruining their lives. He it was who insisted that they wed, likely so that Mistress Boleyn would give up all hope of a future with Harry Percy.

They were all to blame, all those powerful men, and the ones who suffered for it were the two who were innocent in the scheme.

They were all wrong and after all these years of being a half married woman, she had had enough. She did not want to return to her husband, but she was entitled to her place as the Countess of Northumberland. She wanted to be back in the place for which she had married, for which she had sacrificed so much.

She sat down to write to her husband.

***

Harry Percy was more than surprised to see his wife's seal on a letter. He was just recovering from one of his many illnesses when it arrived; it was his first day out of bed for over a week and he had a lot of work to catch up on, but he sipped his ale and gave his full attention to Mary's words. She must have some serious problems to be writing to him, he knew. Perhaps she was dying! Harry felt a little smile form at the thought and he tore open the letter.

My Lord, she wrote, *Having given the matter much thought, I feel that I am entitled to my place in your household. Do not, I beg you, take that to mean I wish a reconciliation with you, as nothing could be farther from my mind, but living here with my father when I have sacrificed so much for the Northumberland title, is becoming intolerable. I am a married woman and should be given the respect and status of a married woman.*

I beg you allow me to move to Alnwick Castle. I do not intend to hinder you or your life in any way, and I wish I did not have to ask anything of you, but I see no alternative.

I am, Sir, your obedient servant,
Mary Percy, Countess of Northumberland

Harry gave a short laugh at the words 'your obedient servant'. Of course, it was the polite thing to write, but Mary was nobody's obedient servant, certainly not his. As to her request, he would have to think on it and he would need to see her first, to be sure of her sincerity about not hindering him in any way.

It could work. The Castle was big enough and it was sadly lacking its Countess. He could certainly do with the help, since domestic arrangements fell to him in her absence and he was not always well enough to deal with them.

Only last week he had to rise from his bed to settle a dispute among the servants about a stolen ornament. Ridiculous, when he had married to be free of such concerns. Anne would have known what to do better than him.

He felt stronger today and would be even stronger tomorrow, strong enough to travel to Shropshire and discuss this proposal with his wife.

***

The journey to Shrewsbury was long and arduous and half way there, Harry admitted to himself that he should have waited a few more days at home before he attempted it. He was exhausted and stopped at an inn for two whole days before he could face more of the bumping and rocking of the uncomfortable coach journey.

He had given no notice that he was coming, none at all and he thought perhaps he should have. He was not sure about his reasons for that, possibly because he did not want to give her time to move elsewhere, did not want to give her father time to arrange to have him barred from the house.

Still feeling unwell, Harry was in a foul mood when he arrived to be met with a superior manservant who had the damned nerve to ask if he was expected.

"No, I am not bloodywell expected," Harry shouted. "Tell Lady Northumberland her husband is here and be quick. Get me some wine as well."

The servant fled while Harry collapsed into a chair beside the door and closed his eyes. He did not realise he was dozing until someone touched his arm, waking him with the requested goblet of wine. It was Mary.

"You should have sent word, My Lord," she said. "I would have had a proper welcome prepared."

"Would you? How touching."

"What else? You are an important earl and my husband."

She stood waiting while he sipped his wine, could not help but see his sickly pallor, the dark circles beneath his eyes and the almost skeletal frame beneath his skin. Her heart leapt with a hope that perhaps this was the end of him.

"Whatever the reason, I thank you," said Harry.

He handed her the empty goblet which she passed to the servant, dismissing him with a wave of her hand.

"Perhaps we should go somewhere more private, My Lord," she said. "Then you can tell me why I am so honoured as to receive a visit from you."

Oh, the formality! Mary really wanted to scream at him, hit him with something heavy, but there were rules and they had to be followed, at least where the servants might hear.

She led him into the small sitting room, taking careful note of the weakness in his legs, the way he held onto the wall to support himself as they walked. He was indeed quite ill this time. Of course she knew he was not the fittest of men, but this was different, much more serious. Perhaps it was only the journey that had exhausted him; with luck it might be his last journey.

She poured him more wine and sat beside him.

"Have you come in response to my letter?" she said. "You could have written."

"I could have," he said. "But I would not have been able to say my piece in writing."

"What piece is that?"

"Only that if you are coming back to Alnwick, we need to agree on certain matters."

"What matters? I've given you my conditions. Surely you need a countess?"

"I do, I confess. Does your father know of your request?"

Mary stiffened. Part of the reason for her request had been her increasing bitterness toward her father.

"He does not, but if we tell him we are attempting a reconciliation, he will be pleased enough."

Harry only nodded, drained his goblet and put it on the table beside him. He felt very weak, very tired and just needed to sleep. He could not deal with any question at this time.

"Can we talk further when I've rested, Mary? I need an hour or two before we discuss things. I fear the journey was more arduous than I anticipated."

And you have been ill. She smiled hopefully. If he were to breathe his last here, in this house, it would be the answer to her prayers.

***

An hour or two was what he asked for, but he was still sound asleep when the Earl of Shrewsbury returned to his house in the late afternoon, looking for his supper. Mary was already at the table and he kissed her briefly before sitting himself on the opposite side.

Two servants appeared with dishes, one maid and one man, and Mary took the opportunity to address the latter.

"Will," she said. "Is Lord Northumberland still asleep?"

"He is, My Lady. I went in before supper, to inform him that it was about to be served, and he woke just long enough to tell me to go away, that he was not hungry."

She nodded, then watched as he left the hall along with the maid. Her father stared at her in astonishment.

"Percy is here?" he demanded as soon as they were alone. "Why? What is he doing here? He said he never wanted to see you again and he meant every word. Why have you allowed him into my house and why is he in bed in the middle of the afternoon?"

His voice had risen and he was half out of his seat.

"Do not let it spoil your meal, Father," Mary said. "And please sit down. His Lordship is in bed because he is ill. Indeed, making the journey was not wise."

"You knew he was coming? And you failed to tell me?"

"No, I did not know he was coming, but if I had, I would not have informed you. Whatever my husband's motive for coming all this way, that motive concerns us and our marriage, not you."

"You are my responsibility."

"No," she said. She cut some of the food and started eating. "I am no one's responsibility. I am a married woman and if Harry wants to try to repair the damage to our marriage, I am not opposed to the plan."

"Does he? Is that what he wants?"

"I do not know," she answered. "He did not have much time to tell me anything before he needed his bed." She looked up at her father with an optimistic smile before she spoke the next words. "He is very ill, Father," she said. "Very ill indeed."

***

It was dark when Harry finally woke, the moon bright and lighting his chamber and a few moments passed before he remembered where he was. His mouth was parched and as he climbed out of the bed, he realised he had slept in his clothes. He was so exhausted when he arrived, he had no memory of going to bed, no memory of anything. He thought he'd suggested something to Mary, although he could not recall precisely what.

At this time of year, high summer, it was late when the sun went down, so this display of starlight he saw from the window proved it must be well into the night. He would not disturb the servants, not unless he had to and he'd really rather not have anyone see him in this state.

He was disappointed, when he arrived down in the basement kitchen, to find a maidservant stoking the ovens. She stopped what she was doing and curtsied quickly, although Harry wondered if she knew who he was.

"My Lord," she said. "Can I get you something?"

"Milk," he said. "And some bread."

He returned to the great hall and waited just a few minutes before the nervous maidservant hurried in with his milk and his bread, along with a small amount of cheese. She looked about her nervously as she quickly put the platters on the table, then turned and fled back to the kitchen. Harry assumed she was not supposed to be here, that she was confined to the kitchens.

He thanked her before she turned and curtsied, forced a little smile and ran out.

If that maidservant was stoking the ovens, it must be past midnight. It was light early, so likely it was the early hours and now his memory started to return, he started to remember what he was doing here. Mary had asked to come home and he admitted to himself that he needed her, but he had conditions, conditions she might not like.

An excellent time to put his proposals to her would be now, when her interfering father was fast asleep. He felt stronger after his slumber and his breakfast, much stronger, back to his old self, but that was the nature of this illness. It came, it left him debilitated for a few days, then it left him wondering when he would see its like again.

The physicians were useless; the only remedy they had for anything was to bleed him, either with a knife or by putting those disgusting little creatures about his body to grow fat on his blood. There was one who wanted to pull his teeth, reckoned it was rotten teeth causing his ailment. But Harry had no rotten teeth and even if he had, he was not about to go through life chewing on his gums.

He crept along the gallery to Mary's bedchamber and went inside. He stood over her for a long time, staring down at her with distaste, trying to summon some ardour for her. But he could not; to him she was just a nuisance, an unappealing nuisance who had been foisted on him, who had spied on him for Norfolk, although she denied it, and had accused him of beating her, which was a blatant and slanderous lie.

To him, that last was the worst she had done. He had certainly been tempted to give her a good hiding on more than one occasion but he would never do such a thing, no matter the provocation. He was, if nothing else, a man of honour. Besides, what would Anne say if he committed such a sin? She would never forgive him.

He had seen nothing of Anne for years, but he knew what was happening in London, he knew that the King was trying to divorce his wife in order to marry her and the knowledge filled him with anger. She was his Anne, his alone. They had lain in the clearing and promised to belong to each other. She would never belong to that overweight, over decorated tyrant.

Harry knew his life, along with Anne's, had been wasted because of the King, and yes, Mary's as well. She had no more desire for him than he had for her, poor girl, and now she lay sleeping, oblivious to her husband's presence, oblivious to his thoughts and plans.

He lay down beside her, making the bed move and her eyes flickered open. It was a few seconds before her consciousness registered his presence and she tried to sit up, but he gripped her arm and held her down.

"What are you doing here?" she demanded.

"I have been thinking about your request and I agree. I need my countess and you need your own establishment."

"Good. So, will you take me with you when you leave?"

"That depends."

"Depends on what? I have given you my conditions."

"You have and very clearly," he said. "But I have not yet given you mine."

He still held onto to her arm, keeping her in place, stopping her from leaving the bed and she had an idea he had not come only to talk. She had seen that look in his eyes before, but not for many years, not since early on in their farce of a marriage.

"Very well," she said. "What are your conditions? I suppose you want to hang a portrait of your beloved whore in your chamber."

She knew she was goading him, knew such words would anger him, but still she could not keep them to herself.

He clenched his teeth together, his fingers formed into fists, one of which raised itself over Mary's head, seemingly of its own will. She flinched away from him, making him recognise what he was doing and he forced his fist apart and used that hand to shove her down.

It was like last time. He forced himself on her, but she would not cry, not this time. This time she only squeezed her eyelids shut tight and lay still, let him do what he wished. She had little choice anyway; he was still her husband with rights over her which she had no power to challenge. But he did not want her, not really. If he had shown her some affection, even if it was ingenuous, they might have had something on which to build. But all he wanted was that Boleyn trollop who was turning the King's head and causing a scandal of unprecedented proportions.

She supposed Harry thought she was saving herself for him, but Mary thought it unlikely. She, like most other people, believed that Anne was holding the King at bay in order to drive him mad with desire and get her own way. What that way was seemed to be debatable.

"If you conceive," Harry said as he stood up, "if you give me an heir, we'll talk further."

Harry left before the rest of the household woke, leaving Mary embittered and used. So he wanted her to conceive, did he? She could not help but wonder what he would do if she did. Would he want her and their child back at Alnwick, or only the child? God, how she despised him. Not for the first time, she wondered just what Mistress Anne saw in him.

CHAPTER EIGHT
Too Close to the Sun

Anne had been in a sort of limbo since she had been noticed by the King. She could not look to the future, as she could see no future, not for her. No other man would dare pay her attention while the world knew that Henry wanted her.

She looked back over those years, how she had dreaded the Irish marriage, how pleased she had been to meet Harry. She would never forgive Cardinal Wolsey for the way he had treated Harry, for the way he had upbraided him before his entire household.

She had not been allowed to see him after that, had no chance to discuss things with him, assure him it did not matter, that they would get their revenge. But that had been then, when they believed their love could overcome any obstacle.

They had no idea then that it was the King who was the obstacle they needed to overcome, the King who had his eye on her, the King who had ordered not only Harry's marriage to Mary Talbot, but the dissolution of her own betrothal to James Butler.

Anne thought then that she could be in control, that all she need do was keep refusing him, and Henry would give up and find someone else to satisfy his lust. But it had not worked that way. Instead he wanted her more and more and people actually blamed her for that, thought that it was she who was scheming to become Queen.

The King's sister, the Princess Mary and Duchess of Suffolk, had much to say about his attempted annulment. A great friend of Katherine, she soon forgot how the young Anne Boleyn served her during those long ago days when she was sent to France to marry its King. She despised Anne now, as did her husband, and might well persuade her brother against his scheme. But it would be too late for Anne, as her reputation was already in shreds and it was so unfair. She was quite content to be Mistress Anne Boleyn; she wanted nothing more.

Now Henry had sent Katherine away, sent Princess Mary somewhere else and Anne was being blamed for it. It was cruel, to separate Mary from her mother, especially now when they needed each other more than ever.

But Henry was a cruel man, a man who would brook no argument, who was determined to get his own way no matter who suffered in order to achieve that and the worst thing was that he had the power to do so. What sort of God would give so much control to a man with such an enormous ego?

"He has failed me, my love," Henry's deep voice came from behind her, making her start. Many men had failed him these past years and that was a dangerous thing to do.

"Who has?"

"Wolsey, of course," he replied.

He strode to the sideboard and poured himself wine, poured a second goblet for Anne and handed it to her. She did not want it, but it was pointless to refuse. He would only tell her she did not mean it; that was his answer to everything, that she did not really mean it. Anne had given up trying to explain anything to him, trying to tell him how she felt. He simply did not believe it; he simply did not care. What Henry wanted was the only thing that mattered and he believed that everyone else wanted the same. It was hopeless.

Her sense of fairness wanted to defend the Cardinal, knew that he would have obtained Henry's divorce if he could have. Why would he not? But she had never stopped hating him for the way he had torn her from Harry, humiliated him, called her a 'foolish girl' as though she were nothing. He would not even speak kindly to them, would not consider their feelings.

She cared nothing for Wolsey and if he should fall from grace because of this divorce, that was the best thing to come out of it.

"Henry," she said. "Can you not see that it is pointless? The Pope will never allow you to divorce Katherine; he is too afraid of the Emperor."

He came and sat beside her in the window seat, put his arm around her and brushed his lips across her cheek. There was a time she would have suppressed a shudder, but not anymore. He had interpreted her shudders as tremors of desire and to tell him otherwise was far too hazardous. Now she had grown accustomed to having him near her like this.

"He will pay," said the King. "I have stripped him of all his offices."

"All of them, Your Grace?"

Anne was pleased to hear it. He was far too high and mighty, had come too far from his station in life.

"All except York. He can keep his archbishopric, but everything else will go, probably to Cranmer. He has been loyal."

She turned away to hide a smile, kept her eyes on the landscape outside. Cranmer was a better option; he was embracing the Lutheran religion, though secretly. Anne had been studying the works of Martin Luther herself and she would be only too delighted to see Cranmer in Wolsey's place.

She covered his hand with her own.

"It is good, Sire. You cannot have men around you who defy you."

"And the best thing," he said, "He has given me Hampton Court."

She turned, looked at him in astonishment.

"That beautiful house? That must have hurt him."

"Likely it did, but think, Anne. It will be ours, yours and mine. I shall have our initials carved into the masonry. They will stay there forever as a testament to our love for each other."

She squeezed his hand then turned back to the view. On occasions like this, she pitied him, this all powerful man. Who would have believed that? But he was like a child sometimes, a spoilt child it was true, but a child nonetheless. He simply refused to accept that there was something he could not have; he thought he loved her, so she must love him back.

"He's taken himself on a pilgrimage to York. Tis the first time he's been there I believe, and he's supposed to be their Archbishop." He paused thoughtfully, then smiled. "I shall send your Harry Percy to arrest him. Will that amuse you, Anne?"

Tears gathered in her eyes. He went from arousing her pity to acts of immense cruelty in the space of a moment. He knew well the humiliation the Cardinal would suffer to have his former page be the one to bring him down. Yet she might get some satisfaction from the irony, so might Harry.

He had written to her that his wife was with child. Strange how such news could still affect her, could still drive a blade into her heart. She thought they despised each other, and it was true they were living apart, but not that far apart apparently.

***

When Harry received his wife's news that she was with child, his first thought was to wonder if it was his. The other times had been fruitless, so why this time?

He wrote to Anne with the news. He did not want her to hear it from someone else and think he was reconciled with Mary. If only he knew, Anne would have rejoiced in such news. She wanted him to be happy and she knew he never would be.

The child was not due until April so he would set out after Christmas to visit. He was still unsure of where to go from there, whether he should grant her request to return to Alnwick Castle. It was likely, after their last encounter, that she no longer wanted that. On the other hand, she would not want her father interfering in her child's future.

These were all thoughts to fill his head and give him a familiar headache. He was never sure, as the years went past, if his illnesses were made worse by his miserable existence.

He had few visitors but those that did pass through seemed to take great pleasure in reporting on the state of things at court. That's how Harry knew that Anne was still holding out against the King and how he knew that he was still trying to achieve the impossible – a divorce from his lawful wife.

If King Henry did manage to find a way to defy the Pope, he would be excommunicated, which would put the whole country under an interdict. There would be no weddings, no baptisms and no funerals. Harry had little time for Rome; he had, in the long, distant past, discussed the new religion with Anne and decided it was the right way. He wondered if she still felt the same, since nothing could be committed to writing; that would be far too dangerous. Harry would be delighted to see England free from the yoke of Rome, but he saw no reason why the whole country should suffer because of its King's lust.

He could not help but wonder if the King really did love Anne. He knew how easy that was, to fall for her, to yearn for her and dream about her, and he knew what it was to be denied her. He would almost have felt sorry for Henry Tudor had he not ruined Harry's life.

Before twelfth night, Harry set out for Shrewsbury. He knew he would have to take his time, the roads being icy and possibly thick with snow in places. He also remembered how the journey had affected his health last time he visited his wife; this time he intended to take much more care, have many more stops and for longer.

And everywhere he stopped he heard more gossip about his beloved Anne and her scheme to take the throne from Queen Katherine.

***

Mary went into labour early on a windy April morning. She had waited for this, waited impatiently, wondering all the time if she still wanted to return to Northumberland, still wanted to be the Countess there. This was his condition, that she gave him an heir. It was the most important thing in a man's life, that his wife should give him an heir and even the King was turning the country upside down for that same thing.

They had begun to call Anne Boleyn the Concubine, a name given her by the Spanish ambassador, and it was said she had promised the King a son if he married her. Mary thought that a foolhardy promise to make and no woman in her right mind would ever make such a vow, but Mary hated Anne enough to believe her that stupid.

Whilst these thoughts raced through her mind, a sudden pain shot through Mary and she screamed. Harry arrived just in time for the birth of his dead son.

***

She was so white as she lay upon the pillow that she almost blended in with the linen. There were shadows beneath her eyes, so dark that if he had not known better, Harry might have suspected someone had hit her.

He sat on the bed beside her, something he had never done before. He wondered why that was; could it be because it was such an affectionate gesture, such a compassionate one? Now his heart melted.

Mary had always wanted a child; instead she had been condemned to life with him, a man she despised, a man in love with someone else.

For the first time in their turbulent marriage, Harry felt the shame of that, but he was still not sure if it was Mary he pitied or the cold little bundle of dead flesh he had seen quickly removed from her bed.

She kept her face turned away from him and he wondered if she were sleeping, exhausted from the ordeal.

"How are you feeling?" he asked quietly, not wanting to wake her if she should be asleep.

It was a few minutes before she turned to face him, before he saw more tears running down her face than he ever thought she had in her. Her voice struggled past a sob to reply.

"How would you expect?" she said bitterly. "You implant your seed in me, then run away and leave me to face this alone."

"I came as soon as I could."

"You knew when the child was due."

"And I left Alnwick in good time, but I took ill on the road. I make no excuses; I should have taken you home with me then, as you asked. I know not why I failed to do so."

"Because you hate me as much as I hate you, that's why," she said bitterly. "There is little point in even trying to salvage this ruin of a marriage. I have vomited the last nine months away and the last three days I have suffered the worst pain I've ever known. I refuse to go through that again and if you try to force me to it, I swear I'll take my own life."

He nodded his agreement. She was right, there was no point, and all he felt at the realisation was relief.

His only heir now was one of his brothers and he detested them both.

The return journey to Northumberland was not so arduous, as the warmer weather was fast approaching. He felt strangely bereft; he could not really mourn his dead son, as he had never known him and had not even been there for the child's mother. Surprisingly, the thought that entered his head was that Anne would not approve of that.

Harry was exhausted when he finally arrived back at Alnwick and had no inclination to read the letter that awaited him, the letter which bore the royal seal.

What now? Was he to be accused of something, perhaps neglecting the borders again? Mary had not been here to send reports to Norfolk, but the Duke might have found another spy.

As to the King, would the man never realise that he was ill? He needed help and if his brothers were as they should be, he would rely on them for that help. But they were not; they were too busy trying to defend the Catholic faith and Harry was very much afraid they would soon be in real peril because of it.

A servant set a flagon of wine beside his chair, along with a goblet. Harry poured himself a drink and when he had drained it, he tore open the seal on his letter with a sense of deep dread. Always he was afraid to hear that the King had grown tired of waiting for Anne and had found something for which to condemn her.

For he would never release her to live a quiet life, not Henry. He was more selfish than any other creature on earth and if he could not have Anne, he would make quite sure that no other man could. That was a fact proven by his treatment of Bessie Blount, once he had finished with her and she had given him a son. He had allowed her husband to condemn her to a life of austerity in a convent, separated from that son. And she had given him what he wanted; Anne had resisted, so her penalty would be much harsher.

But as Harry read the words in the letter, he felt a little smile tilting his lips. It was a command from King Henry that he, Harry, should go to Cawood in Yorkshire and arrest Cardinal Wolsey for treason.

For years he had loathed this man, ever since that long ago humiliation when he was giddy with the future he and Anne had planned together. Wolsey was the one who had destroyed that warm feeling, even though Harry now knew it was on royal orders. But he did not need to do it so publicly, so smugly, a common little butcher's son thinking himself very superior to the heir to an important earldom.

And now the King wanted him to arrest that common little butcher's son. He would have his revenge; he would make the arrest as public as he could, he would treat the once great Cardinal just as he had been treated, and he would relish every moment.

But he needed to rest. He supposed the King thought Northumberland must be close to North Yorkshire, as both counties were in the north somewhere. He could have no idea that they were some days journey apart and Harry had only recently returned from Shropshire.

So he took that time and when he finally set out to obey the King's command, he felt recovered and looked forward to the duty imposed upon him. He wondered why he was the one who had been chosen; he wondered if it was at Anne's request, for she hated the Cardinal as much as he and there was no doubt she had the influence to make such a request.

He had no way to ask her. It was far too dangerous to write to her, or for her to write to him. All he had was rumour, news distorted out of all recognition by the time it reached him. To tell him the truth, he clung to his own knowledge of the young girl he had once wanted for his wife.

Cawood was where the Cardinal was staying on his way to York. It was the first time he had been there, in all the years he had held the post of Archbishop of that city, the second most important church position after Canterbury. Yet Wolsey had not bothered to visit, to let the people see their religious leader. If he thought this last minute pilgrimage would win him favour with the Almighty, he was to be disappointed.

Harry ate his midday meal before he set out with his arrest warrant to meet Master Walsh, who was to accompany him. He wanted to catch Wolsey in his luxurious apartments, surrounded by his grooms and his pages, just as he had been on that long ago day when he had torn a schism in Harry's dreams.

On arrival at Cawood Castle, surrounded by many soldiers, Harry ordered the porter to surrender the keys to him and was furious when he refused.

"I come in the King's name," said Harry. "I order you in the King's name to surrender the keys to me."

"My Lord," said the porter. "My Lord Cardinal entrusted me with the keys and I cannot surrender them to anyone without his consent."

Harry felt his fingers bunch into fists, then felt Master Walsh's grip upon his arm.

"Let him keep the keys, My Lord," he said. "The Cardinal will no doubt give the order when we have finished."

Harry nodded, then proceeded up the stairs to the Cardinal's suite, where he was announced. He had wanted to burst in on him, embarrass him before his household, but that was not to be. The Cardinal came out to meet him and, to his consternation, reached out his arms and held Harry close to him.

Harry's resolve melted. This would not happen before the whole company; he simply did not have the heart for it.

"We have nearly finished our dinner, My Lord," Wolsey told him. "We can offer you something, I am sure."

He led him into the hall where the remnants of the meal could be seen, where the men of his household still sat at table.

"I did not come for dinner, Your Grace," said Harry.

"Then we best go to my chamber," said Wolsey.

Inside the Cardinal's chamber, accompanied only by Master Walsh and the Cardinal's servant, George Cavendish, Harry put his hand on the Cardinal's arm and spoke quietly.

"I come in the name of the King, to arrest you for high treason."

Wolsey's face showed his astonishment, his complete surprise.

"I do not believe it," he declared. "I have done nothing against the King's Grace. Where is your warrant? I would see it."

Harry shook his head.

"No," he said. "You must not see it."

"Then I refuse to come with you," said the Cardinal.

"Come, Your Grace," said Harry. "You do not want us to have to force you out, before your servants."

Master Walsh was growing uncomfortable with this exchange. This was Cardinal Wolsey, until recently the King's right hand. This was not right.

"Your Grace," he interrupted. "You cannot see the warrant because it lists items the King has ordered be kept from you."

"If that be the case, Master Walsh," said Wolsey. "I shall agree to accompany you, not my Lord of Northumberland, who I knew as a wilful page in my household."

And Harry had softened toward him, had pitied him, but he still thought himself superior, this butcher's son who, like Icarus, had flown too close to the sun and melted his wings.

"I shall stay here," said Harry. "I must inventory your goods and chattels, audit your accounts and see that they are in order."

That was when the Cardinal finally gave in to his distress. His eyes filled with tears, his already haggard face seemed to form new lines before the eyes of the men there with him.

"Be of good cheer, Your Grace," said Walsh. "His Majesty was always fond of you. I am sure that once he has heard you out, he will know it is but scandal by your enemies that has caused this. You will soon be back where you belong."

Harry's heart softened again for a brief moment, then he remembered why he hated him and it was not only that humiliating scene in the Cardinal's own household. He recalled when he married, how Wolsey had sent servants from his own household to spy on him, how he had tried to control Harry's life even after he left his service.

Butcher's son!

As the Cardinal tipped his tankard to drain it, his eyes caught Harry standing there, watching and enjoying his humiliation. He had changed somewhat from the gangling youth who had presumed to get himself betrothed without consent. Wolsey had heard many times that Percy was not a well man and his appearance here proved it.

He did not stand, only leaned back in his chair and stared at his visitor.

"How have I offended His Majesty?" Wolsey muttered.

"Do you question His Majesty's orders?" Harry demanded.

"No, no, of course not."

"Good. You will go with my men," said Harry. "They will see you safe to London."

He watched them lead the old man out of the building and into a waiting carriage. He would have a long journey in which to reflect on his failures, in which to regret that he had ever made an enemy of Lord Harry Percy.

CHAPTER NINE
You Are Trapped

1532, two years since the death of the hated Cardinal Wolsey, and Anne had resigned herself to comply with the King's plans. Not that she had a choice; he had broken with Rome, despite the threatened excommunication, he had set himself as the head of the church in England and could grant his own divorce.

That could only be a good thing, in Anne's mind. It was the first step toward the growth of the new religion in England, to rid themselves of Rome and the Pope and remove the parts of Catholic dogma that were corrupt.

There was nothing that would stop this King. Anne only wondered why it had taken her all these years to realise it. She made a huge mistake in thinking she could do what no one else had done, defy the King, change his mind once it was made up.

This year should be the one when he would finally have his way. It had to be, as Anne could stand no more. No matter how much she told him she was not worth all this upheaval to the people of England, no matter how much she assured him that she would never love him as a man, only as a King, he simply refused to believe her.

He wanted her and nothing and nobody was going to stand in the way of something he wanted.

Her reputation grew worse with every passing year. Her own uncle, the Duke of Norfolk, blamed her, accused her of wanting to be Queen. She had told him many times it was not her, but he, like Henry, refused to believe her. He was firmly on the side of Queen Katherine and the Catholic religion, although he was too much of a coward to admit it.

She had heard that Harry Percy and his wife had parted for good and, more worryingly, she had heard that he suffered ill health. It seemed he was often shaky and weak. She wished there was something she could do for him, but there was nothing.

Now she was the number one woman at court. The King treated her as he would his Queen, better than he had in fact treated his Queen during the latter years of their marriage. People approached Anne with requests for favours from the King and while she tried to ignore them, it was never easy.

Her father came to her after the yuletide celebrations. She knew he had been watching her carefully and she thought it likely he was anxious for her to take her place as Queen, but she was surprised when he dismissed the servants and sat beside her, took her hand in an affectionate gesture she had rarely known from him.

"Anne, my dear," he began. "I have hoped all this time that this thing with the King would peter out, but it seems it only grows more intense. Rumours abound, but I need to know the truth, for my own peace of mind and for your safety."

"My safety?" said Anne. "Since when has my safety been a factor?"

"It has always been a factor."

"The King still clings to the idea of making me his Queen," she said. "I cannot dissuade him."

"Anne, it would not be good for you," said Sir Thomas. "Is there a way to avoid such a thing?"

She laughed.

"If there were, do you not think I would have found such a way? I have no wish to be Queen. I have no wish to be married to the King."

"I am thinking your contract with Harry Percy might be used."

"Now?" she said, her voice rising. "After all this time? If I told the King there had been a pre-contract, he would likely charge us both with treason."

"Surely not. He is besotted with you."

She turned her dark eyes on him in a stare that made him move away.

"He is not besotted with Harry," she said.

Sir Thomas frowned thoughtfully.

"Then perhaps..." he began, then stopped abruptly.

"Perhaps what?"

"Perhaps if you give him what he wants, what he has waited for all these years, his ardour might fade."

"He is right, Anne," said a new voice.

Anne got to her feet and hurried to meet her brother, her hands outstretched to take his.

"George," she said. "How lovely to see you. I have missed your counsel."

"Then take it now. Listen to our father; give King Henry what he wants and you might yet be allowed to leave him."

She held his hand and led him to sit beside her. Here she was, her beautiful clothes testament to the King's love and affection, her beautiful apartments the same, her father on one side and her dear brother on the other.

She had suspected her father of manipulating everything to forward a marriage to Henry, but it seemed she was wrong.

"I have considered such a plan myself," she said. "I am just so distressed that I shall be refused the basic right to go to my marriage untouched. That is all I wanted."

"And the King thinks that means you want to be married to him," said George.

"And that is what I do not want," she said. She looked from one man to the other and her mouth turned down. "I cannot bear the idea of sharing my bed with him. I feel no desire for him. He is not attractive to me, not in the least, and, as a man, I do not like him."

"Oh, my darling," said George. "If this be the case, you are indeed trapped."

***

That year, Henry decided that Anne needed a title. A King could not marry a woman with no title, and no woman had ever been given a title in her own right. Some were born with the title of 'Lady', daughters of earls, marquesses and dukes, but no woman had ever been awarded a title in her own right. A countess was the wife of an earl, a marchioness the wife of a marquess and a duchess the wife of a duke.

It was a difficult question but Henry, as always, found a way. He would give Anne the title of Marquess of Pembroke. It was a man's title, to be sure, but he could find no evidence that a woman could not wear a male title and it was a title that was in his gift.

He felt better when he had the Letters Patent in his hand. All that was now stopping him from marrying the love of his life was this question of the validity of his marriage to Katherine, a question that still hovered over them like a black cloud.

Anne had tried to talk him out of it. She had tried to assure him that it was not right, that he should not change the law of the land and the church but Henry knew it was her gentle nature which made her talk that way. She even felt sympathy for Katherine and Mary; that told him she was a most compassionate and wonderful woman, the only woman for him.

Anne was going to make a great Queen, a far better Queen than any that had gone before her. God was telling him so.

This night he had announced Anne's new title and seen her wear the gorgeous cloth and wonderful colours that were not permitted to her before. As soon as they were married, she would wear purple and ermine and she would give him sons; he was sure of it.

Anne could not help but be happy with her illustrious title. Her father was Earl of Wiltshire, her brother Viscount Rochford but her new title put her above even them. She could hardly be sorry for that.

She sat beside the King at the end of the dance and glanced surreptitiously at him. He was a fine figure of a man, despite his age and his increased weight, and his clothes were glorious. Where once she had found his looks unattractive, those looks were gradually becoming more appealing. Perhaps it was the familiarity, the closeness he had initiated. Whatever it was, she could still summon no desire for him.

She had never felt that little tingle, that throbbing deep inside for any man except for Harry Percy. Certainly the King had never ignited such feelings in her.

She had thought a lot about her father's words, about her brother's, and she knew she must give in to Henry. It was the only way to perhaps make him realise he did not really love her.

Other women had loved him, had shared his bed, but they were all too afraid to refuse him. Yet Katherine had loved him; for twenty years she had loved him, genuinely and dearly, but he was young when first she knew him.

He was not so bad; she could certainly think of worse men to couple with. He had done so much to have his way, he had broken with

Rome, formed his own church, turned on some of his oldest friends but Anne did not believe he had done all those things out of love for her. He had done it because he could not bear not to have his own way in all things.

And what else might he do to have his way? He had even turned on Wolsey, would have had him executed if he had not died on his way to London to face trial.

Anne was convinced that if she gave in to him, she would be cast aside, possibly carrying his child, just like her sister. She would go along with Henry; it was the only way to have some semblance of a life.

She had to forget Harry Percy, had to forget that his misfortunes were Henry's doing and hope that giving in to him would be the end of his obsession and free her once and for all.

***

Mary Percy was seeing her father's lawyer this morning and when he arrived, she sat with him in the small sitting room beside her bedchamber and put her case.

"I want an annulment," she said.

"My Lady," said the man. "I can understand your feelings, but do you have grounds? It is a pity that the disrespect you have suffered is not a valid reason, but that is the law. Once married, you are married for life. Those God has joined together..."

"Stop," Mary said, holding up her hand. "I have grounds. My husband had made a previous contract of marriage with Mistress Anne Boleyn. He was not free to marry me."

The lawyer drew a sharp breath.

"If that were true," he said, "it would also mean that she is not free to marry the King and everyone knows that is why he is intent on divorcing the Queen. Can you imagine his anger, should he learn of this previous contract? He might even find some charge of treason to bring against Lord Percy, just to have him out of the way."

"I know that," she said coldly. "But whether or not it pleases the King, it is the truth. We are not lawfully married and I want an annulment on those grounds."

"But Lord Percy's life would be in jeopardy."

"I suppose so," she said. "I hope you do not expect me to care what happens to him. Begin proceedings, please."

"Do you know who stood as witness to this contract? It would help."

Mary's mouth twisted thoughtfully.

"No, I do not. It was some snot nosed little sycophant who overheard them. Wolsey would have known his name, but tis too late to ask him. Begin proceedings and we will see where they lead."

When he had gone, Mary's heart skipped a beat. He was right that it was a dangerous thing to do, to accuse Anne Boleyn, the King's obsession, but she had every right to bring this action if she chose. She had not seen Harry since the birth of her child, when they agreed never to see each other again. They had no marriage, so why should she not obtain her freedom? Anne Boleyn; *Mistress* Anne Boleyn – the woman was not even of the nobility, not really. The King's recent award of Marquess of Pembroke meant nothing.

Harry Percy was just recovering from one of his many illness when he received the petition for an annulment from Mary, citing his pre-contract with Anne Boleyn.

This was the first day he had been out of bed for a week and he was feeling weak and not inclined to deal with something so grave.

Why Mary had waited all these years to take this step, he could not imagine. Perhaps she had never thought of it before, perhaps she had harboured a hope that their marriage could be salvaged and now realised it was a lost cause. She must know this was not a wise step.

He perused the document carefully, noting that she had no evidence but her word. It was no secret that he and Anne betrothed themselves, but one could hardly call it a contract of marriage, not without witnesses.

He wished it could. There was nothing he would like better than for it to be proven he had contracted a marriage with Anne; that would mean his freedom and hers and they might even be able to rekindle what they once had and be together. But, no; the King would never allow them to be happy.

He smiled, a little remorseful smile as these thoughts raced through his head. He had heard nothing from Anne since that last letter, telling him it would be too dangerous to keep in contact. It was possible she did actually love the King by now; he had certainly done everything within his power to persuade her, scandalising Christendom by trying to divorce his wife, elevating the Boleyn family with honours and titles. Who knew what else he had planned? Harry thought Anne would resist even all that, but he could be wrong.

He could not allow Mary to endanger Anne. If it were proved there was a pre-contract, after everything that King Henry had done, and she had never told the King of it, she would be condemned in his eyes. And it was no secret what became of those who fell from favour.

He had to stop Mary, at all costs, even if it meant taking her back and trying to rebuild a marriage that was never much of a marriage to begin with.

***

The King came to Anne's chamber as soon as he received word of the Countess of Northumberland's petition. He was angry, that was apparent, angry enough to charge all three of them, Harry, Mary and Anne, with treason.

He waved a heavy piece of parchment in her face, his voice rising with every word.

"What is this?" he demanded. "Who is this woman to accuse you? Or, are you going to tell me you have been lying to me all this time, that you are not free to marry me?"

As you are not free to marry me.

She caught his hand and kissed it. Appeasement was what was needed now. He was about to set up his own church, with himself as the head; she wanted nothing to interfere with that. To be rid of the Pope was worth any sacrifice.

"Let me order an enquiry, Your Grace," she said. "You know it is true that I was betrothed to

Lord Percy, but there was no pre-contract, no witnesses to our tryst. I swear it."

He studied her carefully for a little while, then a smile forced its way onto his mouth.

"Very well," he said. "We will quash this before it ruins our plans."

Our plans.

"We will."

"I will tell Lady Northumberland myself that she should withdraw her petition and quickly. I am to have a new queen, before the year is out. Cranmer will get me my divorce, I know he will."

When he left, she sat down to write to both Lord and Lady Northumberland, asking them to provide proof of the allegation in the form of the names of witnesses to the so-called pre-contract. It was but a week later that Mary Percy withdrew her petition.

***

It made no difference what Anne said, how much she protested, she was the manipulative woman who had slighted Queen Katherine and enchanted their King. And since everyone saw her as that, and there was no way out, she decided she might as well go along with it.

All she could do now was work alongside him to complete the break with Rome and hope to give him a son. If she must marry him, she would do so, but what would become of her if, like Katherine, she failed to provide an heir?

It was not only his mighty ego which demanded a male heir, it was the newborn Tudor dynasty that desperately needed one. Anne would do all she could to make this year the one that provided Henry with his divorce and a new queen.

CHAPTER TEN
Another Useless Girl

November 1532, almost Yuletide. No divorce had yet been achieved and Henry had reached the end of his tether. He had forsaken all others the moment he set eyes on Anne and now his yearning for her was making him half crazed with desire.

"I am the head of the church," he told her. "I am a free man. Katherine was never really my wife, therefore I was never married and I am free to marry you. We will do it in secret, it will be done before anyone knows differently."

She turned to him with a frown. Her first thought was that this was some sort of trick to finally get his own way.

"A marriage while you are still officially wed to Katherine," she said, "might get you into my bed and then what? You can tell the world you were never really married to me, because you were still wed to her."

"No, Anne, no," he said. "That is not what this is. I consider myself a single man. I want you, yes, I want you desperately, but this is no trick, my love. We will marry, as soon as can be done, and you will be my wife."

"If that be the case, why the secrecy?"

"You know how people will talk. You know how many are still devoted to the Dowager Princess." He leaned closer and kissed her gently. "It has to be this way."

"I am not sure."

"Do you not want this as much as I?"

No! Her mind screamed out, but she dared not voice the thought. He had gone this far, farther than she ever expected and farther than he ever intended. How he realised how much more power he would have by becoming head of the church, power and wealth, nothing would stop him.

She could scarce believe it. He was really going to do this, to marry her while still married to Katherine. But he was right; he was the only authority that mattered.

So she prepared for the one thing she had tried to avoid all these years. She still did not quite trust this wedding ceremony he had arranged, and in secret, yet she had little choice other than to comply with it. The night that followed was her main concern.

She had wanted to go to her marriage bed a virgin and she would have her wish, but sharing her bed with Henry? She had known for years that he would have his own way eventually and now she swallowed her fear and made her way to the altar, where her royal bridegroom waited patiently, looking more resplendent than ever.

And as she made her slow way toward him, it occurred to her that this was the end of any hope she might have harboured that he would one day release her, one day grow tired of lusting after her. Now all she could do was concede to everything he wanted and pray he would not one day turn on her as he had Katherine.

She knew a deep dread that her prayer would go unanswered. While the pair knelt on the stone floor and prayed, Anne's prayer was for her own salvation.

***

The Christmas festivities of 1532 were unsettling to Anne. She sat beside her husband to oversee the banquet, the music, the acrobats and mummers, all the time knowing that not one person present knew that she was now the King's wife. The King's wife but not his Queen, not yet, not until the people of England knew about the marriage and more importantly, accepted it. Anne doubted she would ever see that day.

She deeply felt the loss of her maidenhead. She had hoped to give it to a man who was at least selfless, who knew how to excite a woman.

So far, she had been disappointed, but if Henry ever knew of that, her life would be in jeopardy.

A man so vain, so egotistical, so sure of his own righteousness, had no business being so powerful.

So she smiled, she danced, she sang. She sang with the King some of the songs he had written himself, listened as he sang those songs he had written for her. They were not terrible, but she had heard better.

Her friend, Thomas Wyatt, wrote much better songs and poems, and even her brother George had a more tuneful voice. But her thoughts were her own.

"Wonderful, Your Grace," said the courtiers, and Anne joined in with her own praise. "I thank Your Grace for such beauty to mine ears."

All lies, but the truth could be deadly.

After twelfth night, she hoped for some respite when she realised she was with child.

Henry could not have been more delighted.

"A child?" he said in a voice full of wonder. He placed his hand gently on her stomach, his smile infectious, enough to bring a smile to her own lips. "When, my love? When will he come?"

He.

"Later this year, Sire," she said. "Likely August or September, but be prepared, please."

"For what?"

"If you love me, be prepared for it not being the son you want."

He pulled her into his arms, held her so tightly she fought to breathe, then kissed the top of her head.

"You silly goose," he said. "Of course you will give me a son."

"Why are you so sure? I have no control over such a thing."

"But our union is blessed," he said. "God told me where I was going wrong, living in sin with my brother's widow. He brought you to me, do you not see that?"

No, she most certainly did not see that.

"It is the reason I waited all these years, Anne," he said, "because God was telling me that was the way. It will be a son, trust me. We shan't call him Henry. I had a son called Henry and he died. I do not think we should use his name for our son, do you?"

She shook her head, but made no reply. He would hardly have noticed if she had, he was so exalted with the possibility of an heir at last.

Baby Henry was the only boy child Katherine had produced who had survived, if only for some seven weeks. Then there was that other Henry, his son by Bessie Blount, created Duke of Richmond and made much of.

The King really believed that God had sent her, Anne, to him. In his eyes, to argue with that would be to argue with God.

"We will have another wedding ceremony," he said. "A proper one this time, then we will have Cranmer be sure to declare my liaison with Katherine no marriage." He placed his hand on her stomach once more. "There will be no doubt about this child's place in the succession."

Anne hoped he would be a better father to her child than he had been to Katherine's. Mary was still banished from court, still kept from her mother, still without a plan for her future.

***

The coronation was an ordeal. Anne had looked forward to it, now that she was officially married to the King and had people bowing to her, calling her 'Your Majesty'; this crowning would be the seal to make the people believe the King had finally salved his fragile conscience.

She rode in a carriage, dressed in purple velvet trimmed with ermine, but no cheer went up when first she appeared before her new subjects. She was nervous, knowing the lies that had been told about her, and the silence only served to increase that apprehension.

The velvet and ermine was heavy in the June sunlight and her nervousness made the perspiration begin to spread. She kept her eyes firmly fixed in front of her, tried to appear as regal as possible, but what she really wanted to do was turn around and run back to the Tower where she had spent the night in the royal apartments.

Then she heard a single cheer and her eyes followed the sound hopefully. It was followed by a few more cheers, but not as many as she would have liked. She had no way of knowing if the cheering was spontaneous or the result of threats from the King's soldiers.

It helped that she was obviously with child. The people wanted an heir as much as their King, and the cheering grew louder, but there were also a lot of sullen faces.

The weather was hot and the canopy over her head could not shade her from the sun. Her heavy and elaborate clothing clung to her and she felt the perspiration gathering in little beads on her neck and forehead.

The child within her womb refused to be still. It was almost as if it knew what was happening and was demanding its part in the celebrations. It was a gruelling day, but worth it when the crown was placed upon her head and she was declared Queen Anne.

The past was over, the years of warding off Henry's advances, the years of hoping he would give up and release her. There was nothing to do now save go forward, look to a future she had never imagined or wanted. But she could not help but wonder what Harry Percy would think of her now.

She hoped he would understand that this was not her choice, that she could do nothing to stop it. Her life had become like a runaway coach with no one at the reins to slow it down, much less stop its headlong rush to an unknown destiny.

Henry had accepted without question that, while she carried his child, she would keep her bed to herself. He wanted nothing to risk the health and safety of this precious cargo, but Anne was sure he was not going without his comfort. She did not know who, but she was sure there was someone.

She recalled how she had watched Katherine suffer betrayal at the hands of this man with his mistresses and she recalled as well how she had sworn that would never happen to her. But without knowing for certain, there was little she could do.

Henry seemed content to give up their intimacy, which made her wonder if he had finally given up his obsession with her. She knew it would happen; once he had what he wanted, he would no longer want it. She would not be made a fool of; she demanded fidelity from her husband, but if his ardour had faded, it became the most important thing in the world to give Henry a healthy, living son and heir.

***

Travelling was an arduous ordeal for Lord Percy, Earl of Northumberland, one he would go to any lengths to avoid, but the need to witness this coronation was compelling. If he started out early enough, he could have many stops, lengthy stops that might be enough to soothe him.

It started in January, when news reached him of the marriage of the King to Anne, to *his* Anne. He would always think of her as his Anne, no matter what had come since, and now she was the Queen of England and must be crowned. King Henry had not gone to all this trouble, caused all this upheaval, only to leave her uncrowned. He would want to establish her as Queen of England, would want to convince his subjects that he was, as always, right.

So Harry set out in February, when recent snow was thawing and the hedgerows were icy. He took his most comfortable coach, but one that had no markings. He had no wish for anyone to know he was in London, least of all the King. Such knowledge could put Anne in danger, if he believed she had invited her former love.

With extra money for a small attic chamber that was disused and had not been cleaned in years, Harry managed to secure a good view of the procession that was also anonymous. It was close enough to see Anne's face, to see whether she looked happy, but not close enough that she could see him. She would never know that he was there, that he had witnessed this triumphant moment in the King's great plan.

It had been so long, so very long since his had looked upon that precious face, that as she passed, all he wanted was to reach out, touch her, kiss her sweet lips.

She smiled, she waved, but Harry did not believe she was happy. That might be him telling himself she was as miserable as he was to be kept apart from each other, he knew that, but still he thought she looked more frightened than pleased.

She was with child. That was apparent and it was common knowledge that the King had had his way eventually. It was rumoured that they married in secret before Christmas, and that seemed likely if she were with child now. She would not have given in without marriage, just as she always maintained.

The silence of the crowd seemed to deafen him, as though it were the loudest noise. No one was cheering, not one single person and he could not allow that. He drew a breath, cleared his throat and let out a loud exclamation.

"God save the Queen! God bless Queen Anne!"

She glanced up, but the canopy above her head would obscure her view of him. After that, a few more people cheered, but not many. It was not the loud acclaim that greeted Queen Katherine on her coronation, so he had heard, and even when the King appeared beside the carriage, rejoicing was kept to a minimum.

Anne was not popular. There were grumblings, which Harry could not make out from his high position, even though he had opened his window with great difficulty. It was such a struggle to push it up, he doubted it would close again, but that was not his problem; he had paid more than enough to buy the landlord a new window.

As he leaned out, just far enough to see and hoping no one looked up and recognised him, his heart ached and he wondered why he had made this arduous and painful journey. She looked beautiful, but watching her, knowing she spent her nights in the arms of another man, hurt so much he thought it might be the end of him.

He should not have come. He should have satisfied himself with news from afar, should have kept his imaginings, as they told him what he wanted to hear, not the reality of this.

Who would have thought, all those years ago when Anne had accepted his proposal of marriage, that she would be crowned Queen of England? His father and the Cardinal had said she was merely a knight's daughter, not good enough for the future Earl of Northumberland. Yet she was good enough for a King.

***

The Coronation had exhausted Anne. The eyes of thousands of people, all staring at her, many with malice, had been too much. She had not expected to be popular; after all, rumours had spread that it was her fault Katherine and Mary had been sent from court, it was her fault their King had broken away from the church, it was her scheming that had put her in this position.

It was so unfair, and had she been the sort of woman who worried about the opinions of others, it might have hurt more than it did.

It had been a very long day and she had to lean on the King's arm lest she collapse. He might have taken such closeness as a sign of affection; he likely did, being so egotistical, but she could not help that. If he could not see how exhausted she was, how ill she felt, then he most certainly did not love her.

**

As the year wore on, as Anne retreated into confinement, Henry grew more and more excited with the possibility, nay the certainty, of having a son. All was going as planned, God had released him from his sinful and unlawful marriage, and given him a new and wonderful Queen. Once their son was born, Henry's insistence on that would be validated and none could say he had discarded one wife in order to marry another.

He had announcements printed, he had festivities planned, his courtiers knew he would brook no warnings so none were given.

He was out riding when the messenger galloped toward him with the news.

"The Queen has given birth to a beautiful, healthy daughter, Your Grace. Praise be to God."

Henry's smile faded, his stomach twisted as he fought against the need to vomit, his heart pounded, anger swelled like a monster over which he had no control. Another useless girl!

***

She heard him approach the bed, recognised his heavy footfall and heard her attendants scurry out to make way for him. Did they know, perhaps by his expression, that he was angry? Did they suspect a scene they would rather not witness?

Wiping her tears, she kept her eyes firmly fixed on the little red-haired miracle in the crib beside her. She might be a girl, but she was Anne's girl and she could not take her eyes off her.

A huge shadow formed over the crib, making Anne push herself up in the bed and feel the first flush of maternal defensiveness.

"Your Grace," she said. "You have come to see your daughter. Is she not beautiful?"

Even as she spoke the words, her heart hammered so hard and fast she feared it might bounce out of her chest. Reluctantly, she raised her eyes to meet his as he leaned over the crib and stroked the babe's cheek with the back of his fingers.

She was indeed a beautiful child, but there was something vital missing, her sex. Why had

God done this to him? Was he now telling him he was still walking the wrong path? But no, this was His way of telling Henry to be patient, that all would come if he remained devout.

"She is, indeed, Anne," he said. He leaned across the bed and kissed her cheek. "We will call her Elizabeth. A tribute to your mother and mine."

"A boy next time," said Anne nervously.

"Of course," he replied, straightening up. "A son next time."

As Anne prepared herself for 'next time', her husband continued his efforts to have all his subjects swear an oath to follow him. The Oath of Allegiance was signed by almost all his subject of whom it was required, but the Oath of Supremacy demanded they acknowledge Henry as the supreme head of the church in England. That caused men to examine their conscience a little deeper.

CHAPTER ELEVEN
It has to be a Boy

Besotted by her tiny daughter, Anne was devastated when the King insisted that, as a royal princess, she must have her own household and sent her to Hatfield House.

"She is so tiny," pleaded Anne. "She should be with her mother."

"Were her mother a common woman, I would agree," replied Henry. "But her mother is a Queen and has other duties, first of all being the conception of a healthy son. Elizabeth must have her own household; it will show people who she is, if any still doubt it."

"Why can her household not be here, in the palace. There is space enough."

He clucked his tongue and shook his head, as though she was a spoilt child asking for the impossible.

"She will have Hatfield and a full household of attendants. One of them will be the Lady Mary."

"Mary?"

"Yes. It will show the people even more clearly who Elizabeth is, what her place is."

"But is Mary to be trusted with her?"

That look came over him, that look that said she had gone too far.

"The Lady Mary will be her attendant. It will tell the people the truth; it will tell Mary the truth as well as her mother."

Anne's heart began to race. She held his hand, clutched it tightly.

"Promise me," she pleaded. "Promise me that she will never be left alone with our daughter."

He made no reply, only turned and left the room.

By early in 1534, Anne was again with child. Her aversion to her husband's physical attentions had not improved after the birth of Elizabeth, but she had to pretend. He was a selfish lover, thinking only of his own satisfaction, and she had no other with whom to compare him. Often she wondered if every woman suffered in this regard as she did.

At least she had her sister at court since her husband, William Carey, died. Anne had persuaded the King to grant Mary an annuity, as Carey had left her almost penniless, and she was the only person Anne felt she could trust.

But she would never say too much to her. One never knew who might be listening, and she thought it would be uncivil to mention Mary's rapid weight gain. Anne hoped it was overeating and not some new affair in which she was indulging.

Mary was not a virtuous woman. Shortly after her marriage to William Carey, she had begun an affair with the King, but knowing him as she now did, Anne wondered if her sister had been coerced into it, as she had been coerced into becoming his wife.

In France Mary had been one of the many mistresses of King Francis, but who knew that he had not used his power to bring her to that?

After weeks of indecision, Anne had no doubt that her sister was with child, and God alone knew who the father might be. She wondered if Mary knew herself, but pushed the treacherous thought away as she summoned her to a private meeting.

"You are with child," said Anne abruptly. "Who is the father?"

Mary blushed, ducked her head, her eyes firmly fixed on the pattern in the expensive rug.

"I trust you are not still warming the King's bed," continued Anne, her voice rising.

"Of course not," said Mary. She reached out to take her sister's hand, but Anne stepped back. "The father of my child," she said, "is my husband."

Anne could only stare for a few moments, silently trying to make sense of Mary's words.

"You have no husband," she said at last. "Will Carey has been dead too long to have fathered this one."

"I am married to William Stafford," said Mary.

"You are married?" said Anne. "Without my permission, without the King's?"

"We married in secret," said Mary. "We knew consent would be refused and I would likely be forced into yet another marriage with a man who cared nothing for me. You do know that Will Carey condoned my relationship with the King, do you not? He happily accepted the spoils from whoring out his wife to the royal bed."

"I am sorry for that, Mary, really I am. But William Stafford is nothing; a second son, not even good enough to be a courtier. He is a soldier."

"A brave and loyal one. I suppose that counts for nothing."

"Henry will be furious. Stafford cannot be brother-in-law to the King. I cannot imagine what he will do."

"Surely that will be your decision," said Mary. "You still have influence over the King, especially while you are expecting his heir."

"Why do you imagine I will help you?"

"Because you are not malicious, Anne. I have what you were denied; I married for love. Will you not help me to keep that?"

Anne reached out and drew her sister into her arms, held her close. Mary was right; she, a noblewoman from an important family, had had the audacity to marry for love. Anne could do nothing save wish her well.

"You must leave court, immediately, and never return. I cannot be responsible for your safety if you stay. I may never see you again, but at least you will be safe and happy."

***

In Northumberland, Lord Harry Percy was happy enough to sign the Oath of Supremacy. Like Anne, his loyalty to the Church of Rome had long since diminished, and he believed as she did, that the one good thing to come from King Henry's fascination with Anne was his break with that church.

Harry continued to be ill. Physicians had no idea what ailed him, but his illness grew worse and more frequent. He was often dizzy and weak, in tremendous pain and slept a lot. He would have loved for his brothers to be of the sort who could aid him in his work, but, alas, that was not to be.

Both were fiercely Catholic and Harry feared they might put themselves at risk by refusing the Oath. If they did, Harry was in no mood to assist them and risk being implicated himself.

***

Anne felt she was being watched by everyone, and she probably was. Eustace Chapuys, the Spanish ambassador, was particularly interested in her personal habits and she knew he reported back to Katherine as well as the Emperor Charles V, Katherine's nephew, but she could do nothing to stop him.

He still insisted on referring to her as 'the Concubine', even though she was the Queen. He refused to pay her any homage, refused to bow to her, and still regularly corresponded with Katherine, whom he referred to as 'Queen Katherine'.

Henry was furious with him, but he was a Spanish diplomat and there was nothing the King could do to curb him.

That summer was hot and Anne's growing bulk did nothing to ease her discomfort. She kept to her suite as much as possible and the King postponed a planned trip to France as she would not be able to endure the crossing.

She prayed night and day for a son. Once he had a son, Henry might renew the affections that had kept him enticed for so many years. Since their marriage, his ardour had cooled and she knew she had been right all along – once he had fulfilled his desire, that desire had lost its appeal.

She knew his eye was wandering and she remembered the vow she had made to herself, that she would not tolerate infidelity. But she was helpless to prevent it; she could not even offer him an alternative while she was carrying his child.

She spoke of her concerns to Henry, tried unsuccessfully to keep her temper as she did so.

"I am not merely a man, My Lady," he said. "I am a King with the appetites of a King. Do you want my health to suffer whilst you are unavailable? Is that what you want?"

She made no reply, only turned her head away. His accusation had another meaning, a meaning she could not mistake. To wish ill health on the King was treason, punishable by death.

She ran her hands over her stomach, felt the child move, and smiled. *It had to be a son, it simply had to.*

As the date for the birth of this child grew closer, Anne began to suffer from vivid dreams where the child was another girl, or worse.

Once, she had dreamed the baby was born a girl, then followed many more girls, until she sat with her arms full of baby girls, all mocking their father. On one occasion, she had dreamed that the child was a boy, a beautiful, healthy baby boy, and she was so happy. The King was overcome with joy and swore allegiance to her forever, then the child changed; he changed into another girl.

She woke from these dreams with tears pouring down her face, her fear making her heart pound. *This child must be a boy.*

***

During that year, Henry pursued his plans to finally break with the Roman church, ridding himself of the Pope and his influence, whilst keeping the Catholic religion.

There were many brave enough to refuse to sign his Oath of Supremacy. Henry had declared that the oath must be signed by all his nobles and anyone who held office. Sir Thomas More was one of these men and he saw a way to avoid it in giving up his offices and retreating to his home and his devoted family. The King was not satisfied with that.

More had been his friend for many years and he was a man much admired and respected by the nobility and the common people alike.

People would follow where he led so it was important to Henry to know that he had Thomas on his side. But More was a devout Catholic and refused to sign.

Henry was furious with him, his anger terrifying to see, and he condemned him to a small, cold cell in the Tower to consider further. Anne was even more convinced that her husband had lost his mind. If he would condemn his closest friends, who was going to be next?

This child must be a boy.

***

Thomas Cromwell was a man driven by ambition. He it was who had attached himself to Cardinal Wolsey, he it was who had assured the King that no foreign authority had power over England, not even the Pope.

He knew how to fill the royal head with ideas, notions that festered and developed into full blown certainty and when that happened, the King could tell himself the ideas came from God himself.

Cromwell had been Anne's friend during the divorce and he was as eager as she to see the English Church established and the protestant faith recognised as the official religion of England.

But as time went on, she began to distrust him. The devious way he had solved the problem of the King's divorce from Queen Katherine assured her that he would likely dispose of her just as easily if the King wished it.

The Princess Mary had still refused to sign the Oath of Supremacy, but that came as little surprise. She was devoted to Roman Catholicism, spending hours on her knees just as her mother before her, and she would never betray her allegiance to the Papacy.

But while Mary was banished, she was certain it was her father's new wife who was insisting on the signing of the Oath, certain that without her, the King would return to the church of Rome.

Anne's name was already blackened by rumour like this, and she had ceased to be angry at the unfairness of it. Yes, she wanted the split with Rome, but nothing else. The fact was that once the King had begun to question, once he had authority over men's souls as well as their physical bodies, he realised just how wealthy the church was and just how wealthy he could become by taking the role of its head.

Corrupted by the prospect of such power, he was in no mood to hear that his Queen had gone into labour some four months early. He did not even hurry to her bedside; what was the point?

The child would not survive and he had lost interest in soothing its mother's tears.

***

Queen Anne recovered slowly from the late miscarriage of what would have been the son Henry wanted so badly. And he did not come at all to see how she fared, did not think she might be happy to see him, to hear him tell her all would be well next time.

When she finally forced herself from her bed, her complexion as white as the sheets on which she lay, her cheeks sunken with grief and her eyes red from the tears she had shed, he finally joined her for supper.

Gone was the man who yearned to have her for his own, the man who almost caused a war and changed the religion of his country to have her in his arms. Now he was cold toward her, did not even kiss her, or ask after her health.

Her eyes met his and she knew he regretted his impetuosity in marrying her, in making her his Queen. But he had no regrets about the church, about forcing people to sign his Oath in support of him, Henry, as the head of the church. That gave him more power than he ever thought possible and now there was no one to stop him from doing precisely as he liked.

His famous conscience could always be moulded to suit himself; he sincerely believed that every thought that entered his head was God's voice, speaking to him, telling him what to do. There was no arguing with that.

Anne waited until he had seated himself at the small table, then waved the servant away.

"I am sorry to have lost your son, Your Grace," she said quietly.

After a few minutes silence he covered her hand with his own.

"Twas not your fault, Anne," he said. "We will try again, as soon as you are able."

"Tonight?"

"No, not tonight," he replied. "I have a previous engagement."

"Who with?" she snapped. "Some whore?"

He pushed the table away and stood up, towered threateningly over her.

"That is none of your concern," he said in a chillingly cold tone. "I shall come to your bedchamber tomorrow, if you are sure you are up to it."

"And if I am not?"

"Then I will wait until you are fully able to conceive again," he said. "There is little point else."

She flung her knife down onto the table so that it bounced and landed on the floor. She pushed her chair back as she jumped to her feet.

"I'll not endure this, Henry!" she shouted. "I swore I'd never be like Katherine, mildly turn a blind eye to your infidelities. You said you loved me; you pursued me for years, you risked your soul and you made me your Queen. If you are now not going to respect me, you may as well invite Katherine back."

"Do not tempt me," he said.

He left the chamber, leaving Anne fighting back tears of both frustration and fear. So it was over, or soon would be. His ardour for her had been just as she always suspected, like a spoilt child he wanted what he could not have.

"I am the Queen, dammit!" she screamed at the open door. "I'll not be treated like this!"

CHAPTER TWELVE
From a Great Height

Sir Thomas More had grown so accustomed to his cell in the Tower, he knew every stone, every crevasse, every rat that peeped out from its secret tunnel to visit with him.

He had books, he had writing materials but it was not until the late spring of 1535 that he was allowed a visit from his wife and children. It was not something he had been expecting. Indeed, he had asked Cromwell for such a visit many times since his incarceration here, but had always been refused.

Now they had arrived, excited and nervous and the door opened suddenly, giving Thomas no time to register their presence before his wife, Alice was in his arms, Margaret, his daughter behind her and her husband at the rear.

Thomas clutched tightly to them all, his eyes filling with tears. So this was it; he knew why they had been permitted this visit, even if they did not. It was Cromwell's last resort to persuade him to sign the Oath.

"My dears," he said. "What has happened? You are so welcome, but tis not a thing I can trust."

"Thomas," said his wife as she held tight to him, kissed his lips. "The King has promised you a pardon, promised that you can come home with us if only you will sign the Oath."

His sad eyes swept over her. It hurt his heart to have to refuse her, it really did, but he could no more reconcile his conscience with that damned Oath now, than he could when the King first demanded it.

"I cannot, Alice," he said gently. "You know I cannot."

"Why not? Tis only a piece of paper! God knows what your heart holds. He will forgive you."

"Will he? You may be right, but I will never forgive myself."

They were only allowed a few minutes with Thomas, a few minutes in which to persuade him to go against his conscience, then they were removed by the guards, leaving Thomas to pray in private for a quick death. He knew that his failure to abide by the King's wishes, to accept him as supreme head of the Church in England, was about to try the royal patience to its limit.

He had also heard, during his time here, that somewhere in this grim building, like him, sat John Fisher, formerly Bishop of Rochester. He it was who had defended Katherine of Aragon at the divorce trial, he it was who refused to sign the Oath of Succession, which made Henry and Anne's offspring legitimate and the Princess Mary a bastard. He it was who kept silent on the subject of the Supremacy of the church, just like Thomas.

But both were about to be trapped into admitting their true feelings by one young lawyer named Richard Rich. He had been nurtured in his apprenticeship by Thomas himself, but somehow his ingratitude came as no surprise.

News of Fisher's fate reached Thomas via his gaoler, who hesitantly confirmed that the former churchman was to be hanged, drawn and quartered. Thomas felt his heart about to burst as he prayed that he would be spared the same fate.

On the day the execution was due to be carried out, Sir William Kingston, constable of the Tower, paid him a visit.

"Is it done?" asked Thomas. "Is Fisher at peace?"

"He is, Sir Thomas. I came to put your mind at ease; the King commuted his sentence. He was beheaded on Tower Hill this morning."

"Praise the Lord," said Thomas. "It was a kindness of the King."

Kingston laughed shortly.

"Not so. He did not want him to linger into the feast day of John the Baptist."

Richard Rich, the only witness against Sir Thomas, perjured himself at his trial. He swore on oath that Thomas had told him that he did not agree with the King's claim to be head of the church. Thomas' response that he had ever had a low opinion of Mr Rich and was unlikely to have told him the secrets of his heart, did nothing to save him.

A few days later, Thomas mounted the scaffold to lay his own head on that bloodstained block of wood.

With his final words, he captured the hearts of the crowd.

"I die the King's good servant," he said. "But God's first."

***

The execution of one of the King's closest, most long standing friends, made Anne shudder with fear. Thomas More had been no friend to her, it was true, but did he deserve a traitor's death? It seemed that men were no longer permitted to follow their own consciences; the King wanted to dictate to their souls.

Queen Anne accompanied her husband on journeys throughout the country, where they showed themselves as the devoted couple he wanted them to be seen as.

They held banquets, they entertained guests with jesters and acrobats, they accepted the obeisance of their subjects, they bedded together in further attempts to conceive a son.

Anne's desire for Henry had not grown. If anything, it had lessened since he took little care to preserve what had once been a manly body. Now he was running to fat, but, of course, no one dared tell him that.

His lovemaking had ever been selfish, but now it seemed to Anne that his selfishness had grown. He cared nothing for her feelings, nothing for her satisfaction, only for his own and pretending to be excited by him was one of the hardest things she had to do.

It was almost Christmas when she received a visit from her uncle, the Duke of Norfolk. He had been against her since the beginning, believing she should have become the King's mistress and got it over with, like her sister. What could he possibly know about it? He was a man and, as such, could never understand a woman's sexual feelings.

Despite being her mother's brother, Anne was convinced he would see her dead rather than see her Queen. She was likely right.

He bowed, as he must to the Queen, but it was so obviously a reluctant courtesy, very unlike the sort of respect he would have given to Katherine.

"Uncle," she said stiffly, offering her hand. He briefly brushed his lips over it, then straightened up. "Tis not often I have the honour of your company."

The Duke swallowed hard, blushed a little, as though what he had to say he would rather remained unsaid.

"I have a favour to ask, much as it pains me."

"A favour? Would you not do better to ask your favour of His Grace, the King?"

"Tis no secret that you have the King's ear," said Norfolk.

She waved her hand and sighed impatiently, wanting him to get on with it and leave her in peace.

"Well?" she said.

"Queen Katherine is very ill," he said.

"*Queen* Katherine? Do you not mean the Dowager Princess of Wales?"

He did not want to call her that. To him and to all Catholics, she was still Queen of England and would be until her death. But if he wanted this pretend Queen to grant his request, he had to comply.

"Very well," he said. "The Dowager Princess of Wales if you prefer."

"Tis not me who prefers it, Uncle. It is the King."

He smirked, turned away quickly to hide it. He did not believe for one moment the King had done all that he had done without the coercion of this niece of his. Without her influence, the King would have stayed married to his lawful wife, would have stayed loyal to the Church of Rome. He would believe nothing else.

"She is ill and is asking to see the Princess Mary," he said. "Or am I to call her the 'Lady Mary'?"

"I do not care what you call her. I have to protect the interests of my own daughter."

"Will you speak to the King on her behalf?"

"He kept them apart for a reason," she said.

"Yes, because the Queen would not admit their marriage was false."

The Queen? Still the Queen.

"No, Uncle. I believe he did that because he thought they might conspire together against him. I see nothing that might make him change his mind."

"She is likely dying, My Lady," said the Duke. "Will you not have enough compassion to ask the King for a visit from her only child."

Sometimes she wished they would both die; that might be the only way people would stop blaming her for their present circumstances.

"You are my uncle," she said. "Yet you take their side against me. Why should I do anything for you?"

"You know the cause, Anne, do not pretend you do not," he replied. "Had you become the King's mistress, like your sister, he would have stayed with Katherine, he would have remained loyal to the Pope and to Rome. The country is split, pious men are being brutally executed, and it is your fault."

"I knew it would be my fault," she said.

"Who else? You knew the King's desires, his appetites. It is common knowledge that you kept him at bay to increase those appetites, so that he would make you his Queen."

Briefly, she turned away to hide her brimming tears. She would not appear weak before this man, before any man.

I kept him at bay because I did not want him. I still do not want him.

She dared not say it. Words like that could be twisted, could be made treasonable, and this uncle of hers would leap at the chance to twist those words, to bring her down. She imagined how Henry would react to being told his wife said she did not want him. The idea made her shudder.

"I will ask him," she said at last. "But do not expect him to agree."

"What do they have to do to make him agree?"

There was a note of desperation in the Duke's voice, something that reduced him from his elevated demeanour to that of an ordinary man in the street.

"I think you know the answer to that," she said. "Katherine needs to admit her marriage to him was not lawful. Mary needs to sign the Oath of Supremacy. I can do little without that."

"You refuse then?" he said, his voice rising. "You refuse to help a dying woman have a few minutes with her only child?"

"I did not say that," she said, fighting to control the exasperation in her voice. "I do think you should remember to whom you speak."

He took a step back and away from her, his eyes piercing her with anger and humiliation. That he should have to bow down to this spoilt little girl, this nobody, made him want to lash out and strike her. But he controlled himself. He had no wish to end like his friend, Thomas More. So far, he had got away with siding with Queen Katherine and Princess Mary, because, unlike Thomas, he had signed the damned Oath. For this moment he needed to remember that Henry had made Norfolk's niece his Queen.

"Forgive me, Your Grace," he said with difficulty.

"I will speak to the King," she said abruptly. "I will try. I can promise no more than that."

She watched him go, felt some mild satisfaction at having forced the words 'Your Grace' out of his superior mouth. She imagined how she would feel, to be separated from her little Princess Elizabeth, and she pitied Katherine. It was bad enough that her Elizabeth was away from her, in her own household, but she was at least able to see her whenever she wanted.

That evening was one of those when the King decided he would eat privately with his wife in her chamber. Those evenings were becoming rarer and rarer, and Anne knew the reason, but she had not yet told him her news.

She waited until he had finished eating.

"I have news, Your Grace," she said.

He covered her hand with his own.

"We are alone here, darling," he said. "I am but a man, dining with his wife."

"Henry," she corrected herself. "I am with child."

His joy was not what it had been that first time, or that second, but he smiled.

"We must be careful, sweetheart," he said. "This time you must take to your bed, you must rest."

The idea of spending the next six or seven months in bed held no appeal, but she made no comment.

"I will rest, I promise," she said. "But I have been told by my uncle, the Duke of Norfolk, that Qu..." she stopped herself in time. She almost called her 'Queen Katherine' and that would enrage him. The fact was Anne still thought of her as the Queen. "The Princess Dowager," she went on, "is likely dying."

"I've been told."

He frowned darkly. It was unlikely he had failed to notice her slip of the tongue, but she felt safe enough, being pregnant.

"He asked me to appeal to you, to allow her a visit from the Lady Mary."

She did not call her 'Princess'. She would not make that mistake as well. It was her nervousness that caused the mistake; she knew that her request would enrage Henry, despite her being with child, and his rage could be terrifying.

"Is my daughter prepared to sign the Oath of Supremacy?" he said angrily. "Is Katherine prepared to admit our union was no marriage?"

"I do not think so, Your Grace."

"Then my answer is no. Mary is fortunate she is not now languishing in the Tower, fortunate she still has her head. Other traitors have lost theirs."

"Henry, no! You would not, not your own daughter."

He pushed his chair back and leaned into her, his huge face close to hers.

"Who do you support, My Lady?" he said threatening.

Anne had known for many months, perhaps longer, that the King's attraction to her was waning. Her uncle was right – had she given in to him at the start, she would not now be married to a tyrant who would destroy anyone who got in his way. She would not now he expecting yet another child, born out of fear and desperation, she would not now be in that position she had abhorred in Katherine, wed to a man who knew not how to be faithful.

She despaired of herself, wondered if there was any way she could have avoided this fate. The knowledge that she had missed the chance, made her angry and reckless.

"I do not support my husband bedding Madge Shelton," she spat. "My own cousin."

Henry never liked to have his amours known; he liked to think people believed him a loyal husband.

"She is nothing to me," he replied.

"That makes it worse, then," she said. "She is betrothed to one of your closest friends. Or had you forgotten that?"

"I do not forget. What Henry Norris knows nothing about will not hurt him."

"You think he knows nothing?"

"I know he does, unless you have told him."

He turned and left the chamber, his brief joy about her pregnancy forgotten. When Mistress Shelton came to her a few minutes later, she could not have failed to see the hatred in Anne's eyes.

"Madge," said the Queen. "Tis high time you married. You have been betrothed to Henry Norris long enough."

She curtsied nervously, carried the linens she had brought to the Queen's bed, but hesitated to answer.

"There is time aplenty, Your Grace," said Madge.

"Does the King know he is not the only one?"

"The King, My Lady?" Madge said nervously.

"Yes, the King. You think me ignorant of your liaison with my husband? I shall speak to Sir Henry about his betrothed, see what he thinks about your behaviour."

"I doubt he will care," muttered Madge.

"Get out!" snapped Anne. "I never want to see your disloyal face again."

She was not to have her wish. Madge went straight to the King, who ordered that his wife retain his latest mistress as one of her maids of honour. The humiliation she was suffering now, forced to have his whores to serve her, echoed that for which she had pitied Katherine.

For a long time, Anne had thought perhaps she would be different, perhaps Henry would not treat her as he had his first Queen. He had stayed faithful to Anne for six years, while she gave him no encouragement. He had changed the laws of the country just to have her for his wife.

Could she be blamed for thinking he really loved her, that he would never betray her no matter what? She should have listened to her heart, listened when her own thoughts told her he was persistent and determined only because here was something he could not have for the asking.

Gently, she touched her still flat womb and once more prayed for a healthy, living son. It was the only thing that would save her now.

CHAPTER THIRTEEN
The Jousting Accident

In the north, Harry Percy had finally fallen out with all his family, his brothers and his mother. It seemed they wanted to cling steadfastly to the Roman church, despite how the law was changing, despite knowing it might cost them their lives.

Harry was determined that their stubbornness would not cost him his estates and his livelihood, even if he were no longer here to care about it. And there was always a slim chance that generosity from him might soften the King toward his brothers, although he doubted it.

He spent more and more time asleep nowadays, more and more time with fat little leeches stuck to his body. How strange that such a short time ago he was young and carefree, in love and looking forward to a contented future. When was that? Only ten years ago? It seemed like another life, a distant past life that was lived by someone else.

Now he knew he could not last long, he sent for a lawyer to put his affairs in order and he made a Will, leaving his entire estate to the King. It might just save the Percys, at least his mother if not his brothers.

He had not seen his wife for years, not since the loss of their only child, and even if he wanted to travel to Shrewsbury to visit her, the journey would be too much. Not that he wanted to see her. He had been relieved not to have her presence in his home and he had no doubt that she felt the same.

If she were unhappy, it might make her father feel something of the blame for that. It was a pity that his own father was no longer alive to take any of that blame upon himself.

But it was the King, so he was told, who insisted on this farce of a marriage. It was the King who had separated him from Anne because he had taken a fancy to her himself, because the royal loins had honoured her with their attention. And look where that had led, the whole country in turmoil, many afraid for their very souls, all for the sake of one man's lust.

But he had little choice other than to leave his estate to that King. He would be sure Henry got to hear of it in the vain hope that it would soften his heart toward the Percy family.

***

That Christmas of 1535 was as joyous as every other Christmas before it. There was no warning that this year would be different and Anne was pleased that the King stayed with her, did not desert her for the delights of Madge Shelton and other sluts about the court.

He could not, of course, bed with Anne, since her pregnancy must be preserved at all costs, but he spent the whole twelve days with her, dancing, singing, enjoying the entertainments.

Henry cancelled another planned trip to Calais as he did not want Anne to make such an arduous journey in her condition, and he wanted his Queen with him.

Perhaps things would be all right after all, if he would cancel such an important journey for her sake. He really wanted her with him enough to postpone it; that gave her comfort and endeared him to her.

It was just after twelfth night that news came to them of the death of the Dowager Princess of Wales. Katherine of Aragon, that stately, impeccable woman, that woman whom Anne had pitied all those years ago when first she came to court, was no more.

She felt strangely grief stricken to know that she was gone. She took to her chamber and wept, but she dared not ask Henry to put the court into mourning for her.

This feeling that overcame Anne was unlikely, since Katherine's death strengthened her own position. No more would there be devious supporters of Katherine plotting to bring down Anne and reunite Henry with his former wife.

But despite that, more gossip spread around the country. It was said that Katherine's heart had been black when they cut her open and rumour now had it that Anne had put a curse on her.

She wanted to laugh at that. It was ridiculous, since Katherine was no threat to her. She had tried to make her banishment more comfortable, even pleaded with the King to allow a meeting between her and Mary, but nobody would ever believe that, even if it were announced as a proclamation.

She found Henry alone but for his close servants. He glanced up from his work and gave her a half smile that she felt sure was forced, but she continued to stand beside him.

"I come to offer my condolences," she said.

"On the death of my sister-in-law? Why should that be? She was your enemy."

His sister-in-law. That was so typical of Henry, to pretend those twenty years as Katherine's husband never existed, that they were some pretence that never really happened.

"You made her my enemy," said Anne, her anger mounting. "I always had respect for her."

"She is gone now," said the King. "But do not get too comfortable, Madam. I rid myself of one wife, one of far more importance than you."

"You are threatening me? And I but came to offer sympathy." She touched her stomach soothingly. "Does this child mean nothing to you?"

News of Katherine's death had chilled him, filled him with regret. He had cast her aside, a loyal wife whom he had loved, and now it was clear that God was telling him He was as yet not satisfied.

His eyes wandered over Anne, and he knew that the notion that entered his head was a reply from God. She had enchanted him, had seduced him away from his marriage, had caused him to split the country and even execute his closest friends. Was the Almighty now telling him he had married a witch? Why else would He take his male children?

But she was with child and she could well be carrying the heir, the son he so desperately needed. God might still be telling him to wait, that he would learn that he was right.

He stayed in his chair but pulled her against him, held her stomach close to his face, turned his head and gently kissed the satin that covered her precious cargo.

"Forgive me, my love," he said. "I am distraught. I thought I would be glad to see the end of Katherine, but I find myself strangely affected."

She held him against her, stroked his hair, bent and kissed the top of his head. It would be all right; this child would be a boy and with Katherine gone, more people would accept her as Queen. They would be happy again; Henry would love her again.

Henry ordered an expensive funeral for his former Queen and a celebration of her life took place at the palace that evening. He was very attentive to his present Queen, enough to make Anne feel more secure.

***

They were at Greenwich later in the month for the jousting. Henry was a keen jouster and always took part in the lists; that day was no exception. Anne sat on her Queen's throne, wrapped in her ermine lined purple cloak for a shield against the harsh January weather.

She wore the necklace with her initialled pendant hanging from the pearls and her dark eyes followed the King as he cantered forward, his lance ready to unhorse his opponent.

He had shared her bed last night. They had not made love, of course, since nothing could be allowed to endanger this foetus, which could well grow to be the next King of England. But he had held her close, kissed her tenderly just as he had in the early days, and she had slept in his arms.

She felt better, felt that she would win back his love, even though his love was a thing she had never wanted. Strange that she had never loved him, no matter what he had done for her. Yet those things were not for her, not to her mind. He had done all those things for himself, because he wanted to free himself of the Pope, wanted to free himself of Katherine, wanted Anne, and he was the King; no one was going to come between him and what he had set his mind on.

She had grown fond of him over the years, but she could never forget that it was he and Wolsey who had destroyed her chance of being with the man she really loved. Wolsey was gone, her revenge on him complete, and she had long ceased to want revenge on Henry. It was too dangerous to even think about.

She had no choice but to show Henry the love he craved and now, as she watched him, she saw once again what a wonderful horseman he was. He looked splendid in his armour which shone in the winter sunlight, and she was enjoying the entertainment, laughing and clapping her hands, crying out her joy.

Then it happened. Henry was easy enough to spot, being taller and fuller built than any of the other contestants, and she watched with mounting excitement as he cantered toward his challenger once more. But this time his adversary's lance unhorsed the King, he landed on the frost covered ground, his heavily armoured horse fell on him and the crowd subsided into hushed silence.

Anne leapt to her feet, her arms outstretched as though to catch her husband as he fell. It was an empty gesture, an impulse in the few seconds after the fall, then she screamed and fainted into the arms of her brother, George.

Having revived his sister, George wanted to take her to her chamber, but she insisted on going to the King. What she saw when she entered his apartment, made her feel dizzy again and she leaned heavily on her brother for support.

The King lay completely still, his servants busy with water and cloths, while his groom of the stool, Sir Henry Norris, removed as much of his armour as was possible. Still the King remained unconscious, still nothing could wake him.

Anne moved close to sit on the bed beside him, to take his hand and hold it to her lips. It was a touching scene, one that a few among those present did not trust. Charles Brandon, the Duke of Suffolk, in particular stared at Anne with a frown, a grimace of disapproval, a grimace so fiercely hateful that she could almost feel it.

The Duke was the King's best friend and the widower of his sister, the Princess Mary Tudor. He was one of Anne's worst enemies. He had been a great friend of Cardinal Wolsey and supporter of Queen Katherine and although he had obeyed the King's wishes regarding his divorce and marriage to Anne, he blamed her entirely for turning Henry against his lawful marriage.

Still, she was the Queen and if she wanted to sit at the King's bedside and hold his hand during this worrying time, it was none of the Duke's concern. It was men like him who were trying to turn Henry against his wife, but while she carried his child, they would not succeed.

It was two hours before the King regained consciousness and during this time Anne sat with him, held onto that heavily ringed hand and silently prayed, although her prayers were muddled. Part of her desperately wanted the King to recover; he was the only protection she had against her many enemies. But part of her wished him dead, while Elizabeth was his natural heir and she, Anne, would have a place from which no one could topple her.

The King recovered over the next few days, but his leg was badly injured and seemed likely never to fully mend. He would certainly never joust again, a fact which gave him a sour temper; it had ever been his favourite sport and now it was denied him.

He began to wonder for what he was being punished, began to wonder just what God really wanted of him. He thought he saw a glimmer of an answer when, a few days later, Anne miscarried of a boy child.

There could be no clearer message, for it happened on the very day of Katherine's funeral.

CHAPTER FOURTEEN
Dead Men's Shoes

Anne was depressed, more depressed than she had ever been in her life. She had thought things were going well, believed that Henry's love for her had been rekindled, that it was still as strong as ever. She had begun to believe that his little dalliances with the likes of Madge Shelton and a few others could never lure him away from his wife.

She had been furious with him over his women and if he thought her jealousy was caused by her love for him, it was best to let him think so. He did not need to know that it was the blow to her dignity which caused her fury, as well as the fear that his love for her was fading fast.

Nothing happened at court that its Queen failed to hear about and this new trollop of Henry's was no different.

Her name was Mistress Jane Seymour, sister of those Seymour brothers who had been edging their way into the King's good graces for months. Anne had heard via her ladies that the King had sent this Seymour a purse of gold coins and that she had sent them back with a note that if the King wished to gift her money, he should do so when she had a husband.

Anne could almost find that amusing were it not for her recent loss of a son and the dull dread which assailed her. Mistress Seymour was following her, Anne, refusing to give in to the King. Was her mention of a husband her way of telling him that she, too, wanted nothing less than marriage?

He would not have to tear England away from the church this time, would he? But it would not be easy. Anne would not go quietly; she was his lawful wife and she would remain so. But an irritating little memory crept into her mind, a memory of three years ago when he had insisted on marrying her in secret, and while he was still legally wed to Katherine. She had asked him then if he would use such a bigamous marriage to rid himself of her.

He had sworn that would never happen, that he loved her too much to ever want to be parted from her. She had not trusted his words then and she did not trust them now.

He still called her his most beloved wife, still spoke lovingly of her to others, so what was his true meaning? Anne had no idea and not knowing was worse than anything.

He promised their postponed trip to Calais would happen when she had fully mended. No,

Mistress Seymour might try to play the same game as Anne, and that might get her to the King's bed, but no further. Anne had nothing about which to worry, but she would not tolerate infidelity. She had sworn it years ago and now he must be told.

Today she was happy, as she had asked the King to make her dear brother a Knight of the Garter this year. He had smiled kindly on her when she made her request and George had been a loyal servant. She looked forward to the ceremony, where she would take her place beside the King for the award.

She dressed with care, in purple as a Queen should, with ermine trimming on her sleeves and a new French hood edged with pearls. She looked radiant and knew how to flirt, how to tempt the King. He had not visited her bedchamber since her miscarriage, likely wanting to give her more time to recover. She smiled; that was kind of him, but now it was time to try again for the longed for son.

Followed by her maids of honour, she made her way to the King's privy chamber and took her seat beside him on the dais. George was there, waiting for his award, but Anne was surprised to see her cousin and enemy, Nicholas Carew, also in attendance.

She glanced at the King, puzzled, but he avoided her gaze. Instead he called Nicholas to him and pinned the ribbon on him, gave him the award.

Perhaps he intended to make an exception and give two awards this year. Anne smiled at George, hoping to still his obvious fears, but Henry got up and left the chamber.

He had promised her the garter would be given to George! In all the years she had known King Henry, he had never broken a promise like this, had always given her that for which she asked. Her heart sank. It was true then; Seymour's influence was supplanting Anne's and that she could not have.

***

Harry Percy arrived at his house in Newington Green early that year. He had a few things to attend to in London and he wanted to have recovered from the journey before he had to meet with anyone.

Last year he had put his affairs in order, had arranged to leave his estate to the King on condition that it passed to his nephew. He had never got on with his brothers and recently they had been trying to persuade him to renounce his position in favour of one of them. They said it was to ease his discomfort, because of his ill health, but Harry knew better.

They were against the King's break with Rome and if he did not cut all ties with them, the Northumberland earldom would cease to exist.

His arrival coincided with important events at court, events he knew nothing about for a few days after that arrival. He had, as usual, been forced to take to his bed for those days to recover from the journey.

His servant informed him that Thomas Cromwell was putting in force plans to dissolve the lesser monasteries, the ones that had but a few monks. He intended to pension off the abbots and priors and move the monks to larger establishments.

Harry had little interest in the plan, except to think that it was not before time. He had little patience with religious houses and was secretly studying the new ideas on religion. It was nothing new; he had studied these works with Anne when they believed they would be husband and wife.

When he finally rose from his bed, his groom was talking while helping him on with his clothes. He chattered on about events at court, about how the King was in favour of closing the monasteries and more importantly for Harry, the state of the King's marriage.

"How do you know these things, James?" Harry asked. "Do you have a spy in the Palace."

"Tis common knowledge, My Lord," he replied. "Tis said that Secretary Cromwell wants to break up the monasteries and give the lands and income to swell the King's coffers. The Queen has other ideas."

"Oh?" said Harry. "What ideas?"

"She is in favour of using the money to build more schools and universities and for charitable uses, to help the poor."

Harry smiled. It was just like Anne, to think of those less fortunate, and she was right. The King had enough money and when Harry died, he would have Northumberland. He did not need the monastery money; the poor did.

"I expect Cromwell will have his way, though," said James. "He has the King on his side. But I hear the argument has become quite heated, that the Queen has fallen out with Cromwell about it. They used to be great friends, but no more."

"I hope you are wrong," said Harry, choosing his words carefully. "Cromwell is very powerful."

He said no more. He knew how dangerous it was to voice one's thoughts, although he had said nothing which could be turned against him. At least, he hoped not.

***

It would soon be spring, Anne had recovered from her miscarriage and wanted only to try again. But Henry had not come to her and she could not do it alone. She tried to tell herself that he was being considerate, thinking about her health, but she knew that was not in his nature.

He had mostly ignored her since the loss, and Anne had a strong suspicion that something was happening, something other than his indiscreet pursuit of Mistress Jane Seymour. She sensed that control was slipping away and she could not quite grab hold of it and drag it back.

These things worried Anne, soured her mood and when she found her young musician, Mark Smeaton, standing in the window of her presence chamber, his eyes following her like a devoted puppy, as always, she was disinclined to humour him.

"Why do you look so sad?" she asked, but she knew the answer and could give him no comfort.

"It is of no matter," he replied.

"You may not look to have me speak to you as I should do to a nobleman, because you are an inferior person."

He flushed, turned his face away to hide his blushes.

"No, no," he said hurried. "A look will suffice."

When he had left, she felt a twinge of pity, but her words were true and needed to be said.

She had more important things to concern her that day, first among them being how to tempt the King back to her bed. Wearing her most provocative shift, her most aromatic perfume, she steeled herself to go to him. She should wait for him to come to her; she knew that. It was not her place to seek him out, but he was her husband, dammit!

She made her way to his chamber, knowing that he would not be alone, that he would be attended by his grooms and dressers, but hoping he would dismiss them. She did not expect to see him coming out of the chamber of her own cousin, Madge Shelton. Anne heard a mischievous giggle as she passed Madge's apartments, turned toward the sound and saw the King coming out into the gallery, closing the door behind him and still fastening his codpiece.

Anne had warned her before, but apparently she had taken no heed. She was betrothed to Sir Henry Norris, Henry's close friend, and this was how he respected such a man.

Madge was also carrying on an affair with Sir Francis Weston, another married man. She thought no one knew about that, but Anne did. Perhaps Sir Henry approved of this insult to his manhood. Perhaps he was another like her sister's late husband, William Carey, who closed his eyes to his wife's affair with the King while he helped himself to the spoils and thought himself fortunate. Anne hoped Sir Henry Norris was not of that ilk.

Her rage grew into a monster over which she had no control. She took a threatening step toward her husband, her fingers bunching into fists at her sides, her jaw clenching, her heart pounding so hard she feared it might leap out of her mouth.

Henry stood before her, his face a mask of fury. He towered over her, threatening her with his very proximity. She wanted to move away, wanted to run, but her pride would never allow her to retreat.

"You want a legitimate son," she said. "Do you think you'll get one by giving your favours to others?"

"I no longer expect a legitimate son from you, My Lady," he said bitterly. "You have proven yourself incapable."

"You know why I miscarried last time," she retorted. "Twas because I was so distressed when you fell from your horse, when the beast landed on your precious body with his full weight. I was so afraid for your safety, my terror caused me to lose our son." She drew closer, ran her fingers along his arm. "We can try again, Henry. I have been waiting."

He flipped her hand away as though it were an annoying fly that had landed on him, then he turned and made his way toward his own chambers, left her staring after him, hoping he would come back, invite her to join him.

She hated this, hated having to debase herself like this. She did not love him, had never loved him, but she had grown tender toward him and his rejection hurt. She had to give him a son, she simply had to.

It was a curious comfort to know that Henry was not completely devoted to Mistress Jane Seymour. If he was still bedding Madge, Seymour was less of a threat than Anne had feared. But she had to know if her cousin's relationship with the King was carried on with her betrothed's approval.

The following day, Anne confronted Sir Henry Norris. She was angry, furious with him, with the King and with everyone else who was getting in the way of her ambition. Once that ambition had been to marry the man she loved; now a new purpose had been forced upon her, to be a good wife to Henry, to be his Queen, to give him a son.

She intended only to ask him when he intended to marry, but his words angered her, turned her seemingly innocent question into something that would be overheard, twisted and used against her.

"Tell me, please, Sir Henry," she said. "Why are you not going through with your marriage to Lady Shelton?"

Sir Henry shrugged, his mouth forming a very slight grimace.

"I would tarry a time," he replied. "I am in no hurry."

His flippancy made her angry. He had misunderstood the meaning behind her question, which was to hurry him to the altar.

"You look for dead men's shoes," she snapped angrily. "For if aught came to the King but good, you would look to have me."

Sir Henry's complexion drained of all colour, his eyes widened and he looked terrified. He had good cause, for to speak of the death of the King was treason. He needed to deny her allegation, to refute it firmly.

He shook his head, took a step back and away from her.

"If I should have any such thought, I would my head were off," he said.

There was a catch in his voice as he spoke, as though holding back tears, and he looked about him fearfully to see who of his enemies might be listening.

"Do not forget I can undo you like that," she said, snapping her fingers in his face.

"I do not want you, Your Majesty. You are wrong and if I have done anything to make you think otherwise, it was unintended. What can I do to assure you?"

"You must get on with your marriage," she snapped. "And you must go to my almoner and swear an oath as to my good character."

Anne was angry now, angry that she had spoken in haste and without thought and she was terrified, for if her words should reach the King's ears, she would be in real danger.

She had no idea what to do. She should go to Henry, make sure he knew the words were said in anger. Wistfully, she considered that this whole thing, this whole quarrel with Norris had been the King's doing, for if he had not been bedding Norris' betrothed, none of it would have happened. But that would not save her; nothing was ever the King's fault. In his eyes, he could do no wrong. There was always someone to blame and this time it was Anne.

She hurried to find him, to try to explain, as she was sure someone would have already told him. She saw him leaving his privy chamber and she started to run, wanting to catch him before he went out. He saw her, she knew he had seen her yet he turned away and left the palace.

The argument gnawed away at her for the whole of the following day and night, so much so that she found sleep hard to come by. She spoke in haste, in a flirtatious manner as was her want, but talk of the King's death had slipped in unbidden.

The next day was the May Day celebrations. There would be entertainments, minstrels, acrobats and jesters and there was a great joust for them to watch. It was the first joust since the King's accident and Anne hoped he would not be too bitter about being unable to take part himself.

She would smile today, she would be happy, she would flirt and she would make him want her again. But even as she thought it, she still had that nagging suspicion that something was happening about which she knew nothing.

She had noticed the way some people had avoided her gaze of late and she knew that others fell silent when they saw her coming. It was not her imagination, she was sure it wasn't.

She thought it was the Seymour trollop; she imagined they knew the King was chasing another woman, trying to make her his mistress, and they were avoiding Anne lest she question them about it.

Mark had disappeared as well. Her favourite minstrel, who always followed her about, had not been seen today. She had been forced to reprimand him only yesterday for always being there, with her and her closest friends. These were men like Sir Thomas Wyatt, Sir Henry Norris, high born noblemen whose company the likes of Mark Smeaton should never seek.

Perhaps her words were a little harsh, but they were kindly meant. He was doing nothing save make himself look foolish, behaving as he was. She sought only to save him embarrassment, but he might have taken her words amiss.

She would make it up to him when next they met, give him an extra bonus but make it clear he was a servant, nothing more.

The King was attentive that day, giving Anne the confidence to believe his flirtation with Jane Seymour was just that, a flirtation. She knew from reports that the woman had refused to sleep with him, but she also knew that the Seymour brothers were doing everything in their power to push their sister into the presence of the King.

Anne needed to rekindle the flame, the fire that had caused Henry to pursue her, to divorce a princess of Spain, to establish his own church.

Today he was enjoying the entertainments, especially the jousts.

"Would that I could compete with them," he said.

"No, Your Grace," said Anne. "You need to recover from your fall. Then perhaps you will joust again."

He lifted her hand to his lips and kissed it, sending a thrill of anticipation through her. It was not an anticipation of desire or passion, but rather an eagerness to prove to herself that he was still hers.

Then a messenger appeared with a note, which he handed to Henry. He read it swiftly, his smile vanished, then abruptly he stood and left the stadium. Anne's eyes followed him, her joy of only a few minutes ago turned to fear. He had left without so much as a goodbye, without so much as a kiss. That was not like him, not like him at all.

She was never to see him again.

CHAPTER FIFTEEN
All Their Prayers Will Go Unanswered

Henry felt a shiver of excitement. The news that had come to him would be the beginning of a plan he had asked Thomas Cromwell to put into place. The minstrel had confessed, and he had named others, one of whom Henry loved more than he had ever loved his wife. But it had to be dealt with.

He sent for Sir Henry Norris to ride with him. That was nothing uncommon, they often rode together, but not alone, not like this.

They were a long way from the palace before the King spoke.

"I have been hearing things, Norris," he said. "Things that give me disquiet."

"Your Majesty?" said Norris. "Can I aid you?"

"You can indeed," said the King. He drew rein and stopped beside him. "I have heard that you, my great friend, have had carnal knowledge of the Queen, my wife. Is it true?"

Norris' heart almost sprang out of his throat, it beat so fast and so hard that it actually hurt and he could not speak.

"I suppose you know I have dallied with your betrothed," said the King. "I wonder if you have acted in retaliation."

"No, Your Majesty," said Norris, his voice distorted with the trembling in his throat. "I am innocent. I have done nothing with the Queen save befriend and defend her."

"Are you sure?" said the King. "You are my friend and it pains me to be asking you these things."

He did not sound pained, not at all. In fact his voice sounded as calm as if he were but discussing the weather.

"Sire, I swear by Almighty God, I will make a sacred Oath, I have never known the Queen."

"Come," said the King. "If you confess, I will pardon you and no blame to be laid at your feet."

Norris looked into the hard, cruel eyes of his sovereign and he knew he was doomed, no matter what he said. But despite his recent quarrel with Anne, he would not lie to save himself.

"May I ask, Your Grace," he said, "where you have heard these things? Who has been lying about me, about her?"

"Her young musician, Mark Smeaton," said the King. "He has confessed to bedding with the Queen himself and he has named others to whom she has given her favours. You are one of those named."

"He lies," cried Norris. "He lies and I know why."

"You do? I would like to hear it."

"Only recently the Queen reprimanded him, told him he was a lowly fellow who should not expect the same manners as she showed to her friends."

"You think that enough to make him condemn her?"

"I do, Your Grace." Norris paused to take a deep breath; his voice was shaking so much he could barely form the words. "He likely thinks he is avenging himself on her as well as his betters. What other reason can there possibly be?"

"Perhaps because it is the truth," said the King.

He rode away, leaving Sir Henry to pray silently, but even as he did so he knew his prayers would go unanswered.

***

Anne searched the palace for the King, but he was nowhere to be found. She wanted to know what had caused him to leave her to close the lists, to go so abruptly, so out of character.

She slept badly that night, knowing he was displeased about something, but not knowing what. Perhaps his little Seymour had upset him somehow; perhaps the little mouse was not so compliant as at first appeared.

She had looked everywhere for Mark as well, and failed to find him. She must have offended him more than she realised, for he never missed an opportunity to follow her about, to be in her presence. It was odd to find that she missed him, though; well, not him so much as his music. She would make a point of being kind to him when he reappeared.

The following day she settled down to watch a tennis match. She enjoyed the game, enjoyed watching the interaction, the excitement of the players and the crowd, but she was interrupted by a man she thought of as one of her worst enemies, her uncle, the Duke of Norfolk.

He did not bow, made no attempt to show her the respect due to the Queen of England. That was nothing new; he had only ever paid her that homage when she was with the King, when it was impossible to tell which of them he was bowing to.

"You are called before the King's council," he said without preamble. "You are to answer certain charges."

Her heart jumped and her first thought was that this was some dark game of the Duke's, designed to frighten her. But no, he would not dare. She was still the Queen, whether he liked it or not.

"Charges?" she said. "What charges?"

She knew she had done nothing and a little voice at the back of her brain insisted that this was some scheme to frighten her. She had been too outspoken to the King in front of his courtiers, that was the cause of this. Katherine had always been subservient and meek, but Anne could never be like that, never be the obedient wife. Henry did not like it; this was his way of punishing her, his way of reminding her that he was the King, that he could destroy her with but one word.

"You are charged with having carnal relations with four men," said the Duke. "And with plotting the death of His Grace, the King."

Anne laughed; she could not help it. This was some jest.

"How ridiculous," she said, and turned away with a wave of her hand. But three of Norfolk's men blocked her path.

"The King does not think so," said the Duke.

He was serious; he actually meant it. Anne could only stare in disbelief, her thoughts jumbled as she tried to tell herself that this was

Norfolk's doing, that he was trying to trick her into confessing to something of which she was innocent. It would be just like him; he had always hated her, although she never did quite understand why.

He was her uncle, her mother's brother, and was always kind to her when she was a child. It was after the King noticed her that things changed; one would have thought it would have pleased him to have the Queen as his niece, but he was a staunch Catholic, a supporter of Katherine and the Church of Rome. He obviously blamed Anne for the divorce and the split with Rome, like many people. But it was not true. Henry did all that, all by himself. Why should she be blamed?

Years ago Anne suspected that Henry would not want his prize once he had tasted it, that he would find some excuse to rid himself of her as he had Katherine. Now it seemed her fears had come to pass; Henry had lost interest in her and this was his way of ridding himself of her. Well, she would not allow it! She was innocent and she knew it; she could defend herself.

She drew herself up to her most dignified position and followed the Duke to the council chambers. He should, of course, be following her, but two of his guards did that, which made her feel less confident.

She could hardly believe the charges, the ludicrous idea that she, Queen Anne, would have bedded with Mark Smeaton, a lowly minstrel. Why, it was but two days ago she was telling him she could not address him as an equal, and here they thought she might allow him to be intimate with her. They said Mark had confessed and perhaps that was why, because she had reprimanded him. Was it possible that he was trying to avenge himself on her, telling these lies? But it was far more likely that poor Mark had been tortured into giving a false confession.

Dates were read out, dates when Smeaton had confessed to bedding with the Queen.

"No!" cried Anne. "I was not at those places at those times. The King knows that, for I was with him."

Nobody answered. Then more names were read out: "Sir William Brereton..."

"I hardly know him!" interrupted Anne.

The speaker carried on reading as though she had not spoken.

"Sir Henry Norris, with whom you plotted against the King's person."

Anne was shaking her head, searching her mind for anything that could have made the King think she might be guilty of any of these things. Of course; the argument with Norris about his marriage. She had known at the time that her words were dangerous, yet they meant nothing; they were said in anger.

"Sir Thomas Wyatt..."

"He is my friend, nothing more."

"Viscount Rochford..."

Anne took a step back, clutched the cabinet beside her, her heart racing. Tears brimmed in her eyes now, but she found no sympathy in her uncle, nor did she expect any.

"He is my brother!" she cried. "My brother. How can I have committed adultery with him? That would be incest."

Then she saw the faces of the men, saw one or two of them nodding. She was being charged with incest?

"What evil mind has reported such a thing?" said Anne. "Because I love my brother, because he is my best friend and confidante, some foul minded, jealous rival thinks there must be something unclean in it. Was this Mark, too?"

There were a few nods, involuntary nods as they had no real intention of replying, of satisfying her curiosity.

"All these men have been taken to the Tower," said the Duke of Norfolk. "Now you are to join them to await your trial."

She wanted to argue, wanted to give her side of things, but she was trembling, shaking so much she could not speak. Her teeth were chattering, although the May sunshine shone through the windows and warmed the chamber. She felt the dampness under her arms and beneath her bosom, she felt all colour drain from her face.

Anne wondered why this was happening, wondered what she had done that someone would tell such lies about her. She did not believe Mark had invented these tales; he was not bright enough. They must have hurt him, must have tortured him, promised him his freedom if he complied.

It was Cromwell, it had to be. But their argument about the funds from the monasteries was hardly enough to make him want to destroy her so utterly. It had to be the King, but did Henry really believe these terrible tales? Could he? Nothing happened without the King's orders and consent, so he must do, he must believe these lies.

She had to see him; she had to convince him of her innocence. If he believed she had betrayed him with so many, even with her own brother, he must have been devastated. He needed her, needed her solace and her assurance.

"I want to see the King," she said through an ache in her throat. "I want to see my husband."

"The King will not see you," said the Duke. "These are his orders."

Of course he would not see her. Did he see Katherine once he had dismissed her from his sight, despite her pleas for an audience? Did he see Sir Thomas More once he had condemned him?

She knew Henry, knew him well, and she knew that if he really believed the things they were saying, he would hide himself away, bury his shame beneath his bedcovers and stay there. But he had gone out, she saw him go that very morning. So no, he did not believe these ludicrous tales; they were merely convenient.

She always suspected he would get rid of her one day; she never thought he would use such a craven method.

He would not see Anne, and that fact told her that her end was in sight. She had always known that, like all bullies, the King was an emotional coward. Oh, he was brave enough on the battlefield; that was expected of him, but when it came to dealing with the pain he might have caused, he would give his orders then leave the dirty business of carrying them out to others, while he forgot those he had condemned. He was likely out hunting, or visiting with the Seymour trollop, while his wife, the woman to whom he had promised eternal devotion, the woman for whom he had torn the nation apart, was given no opportunity to even plead her case before him.

She was silent in the barge as it made its way from Greenwich to the Tower, her mind busy with ways she could persuade the King that he still loved her. And she was afraid that they would take her through that gate below St Thomas' Tower, the one that people were calling 'Traitors' Gate'. But she was still a Queen and when they arrived, she took the hand of Sir William Kingston, the constable of the Tower, to help her onto dry land.

She wanted to ask him if she was going to a prison cell, but she was afraid of what he would say. She had her answer when they led her through to the private entrance and the royal apartments, the same apartments where she had been housed whilst awaiting her coronation, less than three years ago.

It was such a brief time. Anne had returned from France, fallen in love with Harry Percy, had her heart broken by powerful men, been pursued by the King of England and crowned Queen, all in the space of some eight years.

She recalled her first glimpse of Katherine, how she had pitied her, how it had occurred to her that she would never want to be in her place.

Yet here she was, in that very place, but in more danger than Katherine could ever have been.

There were only three years since her marriage to Henry, since he had married her in secret because he could wait no longer, married her whilst still legally wed to Katherine. She wondered then if he would use it to break his vow when it suited him, had even challenged him with it.

Never, was what he had told her. Never would he betray her. He would love her forever, she had his word, he swore to it. She could remind him of that, if she were ever allowed to see him, to speak to him. But that was likely why that would not be allowed, because Henry did not like to be challenged, did not like to be reminded of his past promises. He would doubtless find some excuse to forsake those promises and he would be sure it was God's will.

As the small party entered the royal apartments, several unfamiliar ladies curtsied. She knew none of them, none save one, her aunt, Lady Boleyn, another relative who despised her.

She spun around, glared at the Duke.

"Where are my ladies?" she demanded.

"Your household has been broken up," he replied. "These are the attendants the King has approved."

She turned away, sank down into a window seat and tried to concentrate on the view outside the window. Henry had chosen these women, or Cromwell had, to report back to him everything she did or said. There was no other explanation for him giving to attend her not only strangers, save an aunt who was almost as much of an enemy as the Duke himself.

Her household had been disassembled and that could only mean one thing; she had already been found guilty.

She would not look up until she heard the two men leave.

***

Harry Percy heard the news from his servants; the Queen had been arrested for high treason. The details of the charges included adultery and incest, as well as plotting the death of the King.

Harry's lip began to tremble as he dismissed his servant and turned away. His heart almost stopped, not only because of the ludicrous nature of the charges, but because he knew that, as the Earl of Northumberland, he would be called upon to sit on the jury that would condemn her. And condemn her they must, because that was what the King wanted and they all knew well what happened to people who defied the King.

Harry's health had worsened greatly this past year and he could only hope to be too ill to have anything to do with the proceedings.

He lay down on his bed, stared up at the heavily embroidered canopy above his bed, and felt the tears gathering about his ears and soaking his hair at the nape. He could not help it; the idea of his beautiful Anne, locked up in the Tower, unfairly judged by a panel of her enemies, was just too much.

If only they had been left alone to marry, to build a household and a family, as they wanted, she would be safe now. If only that overweight, over-decorated, lecherous King, with more power than any one man should be allowed, had not taken a fancy to her, they could have led a happy life together, far from London and the interference of ambitious men.

Harry felt that if anyone would like to murder the King, it was him. Between the King and Wolsey, his life had been ruined and now he found that Anne's, too, was left in tatters. He had drawn solace, all these years, from assuring himself that at least she was happy, even if he was not. Now even that small comfort was to be ripped away from him.

He did not expect to live for much longer; he was in so much pain most of the time, life was hardly worth living and he knew of one person who would celebrate on his death, his wife, Mary.

They had not met in years, but she was still his countess and would still have inherited a fortune on his death, which was one reason he had tied up his estate so that it all went to the King. There were other reasons, mainly his brothers. He wanted neither one of them to have the title and estate; he disliked them both but their adherence to the Pope and the old religion was enough to make him cut them out of his life.

He wanted to help Anne, but there was nothing he could do. He knew she was innocent; he had no evidence for that, none whatever, but he felt it. The crimes for which she would stand trial for her life were crimes which she could never have committed.

Harry was still grieving the injustice when he received a visit from a close and long standing acquaintance from the north of England, Sir Reynold Carnaby. Harry was surprised when his servant announced Sir Reynold; thinking quickly, he could find no reason for such a visit, unless the man was in London for some business of his own and thought to pay his respects.

He was soon to learn that he was not to be spared involvement in the King's latest schemes.

The two men shook hands, wine was offered and they sat. All the time Sir Reynold showed hesitation in his expression and body language, but Harry was in no mood to placate him, to help him. If he had something specific to say, he needed to say it and be gone.

"I have come," said Sir Reynold, "on the orders of Secretary Cromwell."

"Ah," said Harry. "And just what does Master Secretary want with me?"

"You have heard, of course, that Queen Anne has been arrested, that she resides in the Tower awaiting trial on charges of treason."

"I would have to be deaf and blind not to have heard," snapped Harry.

He was still churning inside about Anne's present predicament and did not feel like discussing the subject with anyone, certainly not a man who came to him on orders from the King's little puppy dog. If he broke down before this man, the whole of the court would know about by sunset and Harry would find himself charged with sympathising or some such rubbish. He might even join the other unfortunate and innocent men accused with Anne.

"The King wants his marriage to the Lady Anne annulled," said Sir Reynold.

"Does he? Tis bewildering how marriages seem to be easily erased when they no longer suit."

Sir Reynold must have sensed some deep feeling in Harry, for his tone lowered to one of empathy and he reached out a hand to cover that of his host. Harry made no move to withdraw, merely let his eyes settle on the hand that held his.

"If it can be proved that the marriage was never lawful, was no marriage, it could save the lady's life."

Harry stared at him in disbelief. He had always had a talent for sensing when someone was lying and that talent came to his aid now. He was being lied to and he knew it.

"Sir Reynold," he said, "the Queen is under arrest for high treason; her so-called accomplices are under arrest with her. The King would look very silly now if he were to release her and declare he was never married to her. Just what do you want of me, Sir?"

"Secretary Cromwell thinks of the pre-contract you had with the Queen before she married King Henry. He needs your evidence to prove it."

Harry rarely flew into a rage; such a thing used up too much energy. But now he slammed his goblet onto the side table, splashing red wine into the air and over his guest. He jumped to his feet, his cheeks growing a deep red with the fury which overcame him.

"Four years ago, my wife started a petition on the same grounds. There was an enquiry then, an enquiry ordered by the King himself, and I responded to that petition, before the Archbishops York and Canterbury, as well as the Duke of Norfolk. I swore on oath and took the sacrament to show that there was no such contract." He paused to take a deep breath, to try to calm his temper. "It suited the King then to believe me. I cannot be held accountable if the same does not suit him now."

He went to the door and called his servant.

"Please show Sir Reynold out," he ordered. "And do not disturb me again."

When his visitor had left, he sat at his desk with quill and ink and repeated his statement in a letter to Secretary Cromwell. He considered it prudent, however, to omit any reference to the King.

***

Anne said little for the first day. Her mind was too busy for speech, too crowded with thoughts of how she came to be here and when she looked about the apartments, she remembered being here before, awaiting her coronation.

That was less than three years ago, when the King had loved her, or said he did. She was expecting their first child and he was ecstatic, so sure it would a son. But it was not a son, it was Elizabeth.

Anne's heart skipped a beat as the image of that little girl crept into her mind, replacing all others. She was so pretty, so dear, the most important person in Anne's life and she longed to hold her in her arms, to kiss her sweet cheeks, to hold her close. But she would never be allowed to do that again, and what would become of Elizabeth when her mother was no more? The memory of what happened to the Princess Mary, Henry's elder daughter, was vivid. He had stripped her of her status, of her titles, disassembled her household and put her in Elizabeth's, made her little more than a servant to her younger half sister. He had declared her to be illegitimate, having made much of her all her life. Anne could expect no better treatment for Elizabeth.

Henry might send his wife to a nunnery, but that would bring her no closer to her little daughter.

She caught back a sob. No, Henry would not want to do that. He would want to erase her altogether, pretend she never existed. That way he could salve his almighty conscience, would never have to think about his interference in her life, how he had pursued her, married her, torn her away from the man she really loved, just to satisfy his lust.

She had to see him! That was the only way out of this. He had done all those things for her, he must have loved her. It was not merely lust, not just a petulant child wanting his own way at all costs, surely not.

If she could see him, talk to him, tell him she loved him, his ego would not be able to resist. She had never told him she loved him, never once, not even in the throes of the passion that he was able to ignite on rare occasions. She never told him because it was not true; she had no love for him, but there was no need for him to know that.

She sent for Master Kingston.

"I wish to see the King, my husband," she said. "Will you send a message for me?"

He made no reply for a few seconds, then he gave her a quick bow.

"I will do my best, Your Grace," he said quietly.

That did not sound very encouraging, Anne thought. But perhaps he had no authority and had to go through other channels, Cromwell probably. Was her future now in the hands of a man who was once her friend? Or a man who was once her lover?

She turned back to glance around the chamber at the ladies who sat at their embroidery, all except one. Lady Boleyn, her hated aunt, who sat with a prayer book, muttering beneath her breath, as though her display of piety might make Anne believe she was here to comfort her.

Images filled Anne's mind, images of the last three years and how she had been the centre of court life, how she had flirted with every man, as was her way. It was a trait Henry had loved about her once, a trait that had attracted him. But what he loved in a mistress, he disliked in a wife.

It was with the King's approval that she had given money to his courtiers, and now he would use that generosity against her, he would say she must be intimate with men to give them money. He knew that was a lie, he just knew it.

"You know what I told Sir Francis Weston," she said suddenly. "I told him he was spending more time with my cousin, with Madge, that he was with his wife. And do you know what he said?" Her voice had risen hysterically, but no one tried to stop her. Of course not; they were here to report her words to Cromwell. "He said there was one whom he cared for more than either of those ladies, and that was me!" She laughed wildly. "Can you imagine that? They all loved me, you know, every single one of them. They were all madly in love with me, including the King." She turned to stare at the grey towers outside the window. "I shall soon be released. What can happen to someone who is so well loved?"

hat very day, Sir Francis Weston was arrested.

***

Sir William Kingston wore an embarrassed expression when he arrived in the royal apartments that morning, a look that told Anne he would rather not be the one to convey this message.

"I am sorry, Your Majesty," he said. "His Grace refuses to see you."

"His Grace, the King?" she snapped. "Or His Grace, Thomas Cromwell?"

Kingston flushed, reached out a hand to her, but stopped before he made contact. He wanted to stop her tongue, before she said too much, but he had no right to touch her, no right at all. She was still the Queen, though not for long. Her words were treason and they would soon be relayed to Master Cromwell.

"Your Majesty, please, be careful," he said quietly, too quietly for her ladies to hear.

"I knew it," said Anne. "He does this; have you noticed? Once he has decided he is right, he has finished with someone, he will never give them the opportunity to change his mind."

She turned to the narrow window, stared out once more at those grey and dismal towers, and she wondered why she was here, wondered what she had done to deserve this. Nothing, that was what, and the charges against her, against her friends were ludicrous. She knew it and the King knew it and likely more importantly, Cromwell knew it. She fervently prayed that one day, that scheming upstart would feel the axe upon his own neck.

But he dared do nothing without the King's consent, so Henry must be behind this offence to justice. It was only last year that he had sobbed in her arms when his sister, Mary, had died. He turned to Anne then for comfort, but there was no comfort for her now, no one who might be on her side.

The truth of it occurred to her then and she wondered why it had taken so long to do so. She spun around, her eyes wide as they met those of Master Kingston who stood in the same place.

"I know what he is doing!" she declared. "This is because we fought, because I yelled at him in front of his trollop, Seymour. He is doing this to teach me a lesson, that is all. He is doing all this just to frighten me into behaving like a meek simpleton."

She sighed deeply, a little smile crept over her mouth and she nodded as she sank down into the window seat.

"I can play his game," she said. "I'll write to him, that's what I'll do. Bring me a quill and some paper."

Anne sat at the little desk in the corner of her chamber, straightened the paper and took up the quill, dipped it in the ink, then she realised that the eyes of everyone here were on her, boring into her like demons wanting a part of her soul.

She trusted none of them; they were not her friends, not her ladies, and this letter was private, between a husband and wife. But would an ordinary wife be writing to her husband to beg for her life? She would not.

Had she married Harry Percy, she would not now be trying to justify crimes that had never been committed. No, she would be that ordinary wife, a wife who was well loved and happy, prepared to grow old with a man she adored.

A memory of his dear face crept into her mind, his kind, loving eyes, his playful smile and that slim, tempting body. She wondered how he looked today after all the illnesses she had heard tell of.

But she must not think of him now. She must think of that other Henry, that royal Henry, her husband, who had gone to great lengths to intimidate her, make her believe she was in danger so that she would be forced to beg for her life.

But if that were true, he would have given her a chance to beg for her life, would he not? If her subservience was his aim, he would not have refused to see her.

Tears filled her eyes as she began to write, but her hand shook so much she could not form the letters. She looked up at the ladies who witnessed her every move.

"Leave me, please," she said evenly. "I wish some privacy."

Some of the ladies dropped their eyes to their feet, all except one.

"We are not permitted to leave you alone, Your Grace," said Lady Boleyn. "It is the King's order."

"It is Cromwell's order!" snapped Anne. She drew a deep breath. "Very well."

She bent her head low and covered the paper with her hand, a hand that still shook.

Your grace's displeasure and my imprisonment are things so strange to me, that what to write, or what to excuse, I am altogether ignorant.

That was as far as she got. Her hand was shaking so much, her heart beating so wildly, her pulse bouncing so that she could almost see it beneath the skin in her wrist. She gathered up the paper, flung the quill so that it pierced the wooden surface.

"Find me a scribe," she said, standing up. "And quickly."

***

The letter the scribe finally produced was lengthy and, after declaring Anne's innocence, begged the King not to allow to suffer those innocent men who were arrested with her.

By declaring the innocence of those men, Anne was effectively telling the King that she knew he was taking some revenge on her alone, that he knew well she was innocent of the charges. But she doubted he would listen.

She spent many days in silence, saying nothing to anyone and eating nothing. She would watch from the window, think about the poor souls imprisoned in less luxurious surroundings behind those tiny windows, and know that from this place there was no escape.

She was satisfied with the letter and if Henry ever saw it, it might just be enough to touch his heart. It might be enough to remind him of what she had once meant to him, when he was prepared to go to any lengths to have her, when he would give her anything, except her freedom. Anne had no idea when Henry first noticed her, when he first decided he wanted her, but she knew only too well that, from that moment, she was captured and could never escape, never be free again.

But he might never see her letter. She was sure Thomas Cromwell would receive it, would read it, would decide whether the King should see it. It was a risk; if Henry ever discovered that Cromwell was keeping things from him he would not be best pleased. Cromwell might tell himself it was to save the King more heartache, but Anne knew what it really was. Among those innocent men were those whom Secretary Cromwell had made an enemy of, would value the opportunity to rid himself of.

Poor Mark did not stand a chance. He was a fragile soul, humble and besotted. She could not fathom why he had confessed as he had, possibly because he liked the idea that someone might think him dear enough to the Queen to share her bed. It would be like him and he would never realise the danger such a confession would cause to both him and her.

She was most surprised that Sir Henry Norris was here, accused with her. She knew it was because of that argument she had so carelessly had with him, but he had known the King since childhood. They had always been close friends; surely he would not take Norris' life, surely not.

But there had been other close friends. Sir Thomas More was one. He and the King had always been close, had dined together, talked together till long into the night. It had not stopped him from separating More's head from his body and again, once he had decided on a trial for Sir Thomas, he had refused to see him again.

Even his own daughter, the Princess Mary, he had banished from court. Anne disliked Mary with all her soul, as Mary disliked her, and had never regretted anything that happened to her. Now she realised for the first time just how cruelly her father had treated her. She had been Princess of Wales, the only girl ever to wear the title in her own right; she had been the heir to the throne, feted all over Europe by important princes wanting to join with her in marriage.

Then one day she had lost her title, her status and been forced to serve her half sister, recognise Elizabeth as the true heir to the throne. And no matter how she begged in many letters, Henry would not allow her to return to court. He needed her to sign the Oath of Supremacy, to recognise him as the head of the church in England, and that was something the fiercely Catholic Mary could never do.

If Anne failed to survive this crisis, her little Princess Elizabeth would be treated the same, because she was a girl, because her father wanted sons, not useless girls.

But he did not mean it! He intended this only to frighten her, nothing more. She knew it! Henry loved her; such a great love as his for Anne could not simply turn to hatred overnight. Surely she was right.

She lay down on her bed, turned her back to the curious eyes that never gave her a moment's solitude, and quietly wept.

CHAPTER SIXTEEN
I have A Little Neck

At his house in Newington Green, Harry Percy drank far more than he should have. He was already feeling dizzy and now he wanted only to sleep the day away. That was just as well; his beloved Anne was imprisoned and would soon be tried for her life, a trial that was deemed to have but one outcome. She had no chance of a fair trial, not when the King himself had already decided her fate.

Harry's servants were very efficient at bringing him the latest news and gossip from court and he had been told that the King had sent to France for a swordsman to behead his Queen, as soon as she was arrested. He had no intention of even considering that she might be found not guilty; of course not. That outcome did not suit him, not one little bit.

Harry wondered if Anne knew and if she did, did the knowledge plunge her into deeper depths of despair, to know that it was all pointless, that she was already condemned?

Now he sat beside his open window and clutched in his hand the letter he had dreaded, the summons that ordered him, Harry Percy,

Earl of Northumberland, to attend on the day of the Queen's trial and form part of the jury.

He could see why he was being asked and it had nothing to do with his status as one of the most important Earls in the country. It was to do with Henry Tudor and his vicious need to punish everyone who had ever loved her, everyone except himself.

But the King had never loved her. He had only wanted her, lusted after her and he had interfered in her life, used her for his own selfish needs and now he would condemn her to death, knowing full well that she was innocent. God, how he loathed that man!

There could be but few motives for the King's choice of Northumberland for this task, malice, spite, hatred. But was his hatred greater for Harry, or for Anne? It was certain that both would be hurt by Harry's presence at the trial, and that was just what the King wanted.

He drank some more, sought oblivion in the alcohol and wondered if there was any way out.

***

They had all been judged guilty, all the men who had been tried. Sir Francis Weston, Sir William Brereton, Sir Henry Norris, even poor Mark Smeaton. Sir Thomas Wyatt had been released without charge, probably because his father was such a good friend of the King. There could be no other reason, for had he faced the same, unfair trial as the others, he, too, would have been now awaiting death.

Anne's brother was to be tried later, in the Tower's great hall, but not with his sister. It was quite pointless now to have any sort of sham trial for her, since if she were proven innocent, then so must those poor gentlemen already condemned. Their guilt meant her guilt and there was no escape from that verdict. George might yet have a chance; what law made it incest to be close to one's brother? King Henry's law, obviously.

While his Queen, his wife, the woman he professed to love, awaited her fate, accused of adultery, the King seemed to be enjoying himself. Anne heard from whispers among her attendants that he had been seen out riding, hunting, at balls, dancing with his Seymour slut, without a single word or look of grief or shame.

That told her, if she was still in any doubt, that he knew full well that Anne was guiltless. What man, believing his wife had shared herself with other men, would be enjoying life so well? The charges made him a cuckold, and that was something against which Henry would ever protest. But he did not and Anne knew why; because he knew it was all an evil lie.

She was not alone in her belief. It came to her ears that the Spanish ambassador, Chapuys, ever her enemy, had remarked that he never knew a man to wear a pair of horns so happily. Even he knew she was innocent.

"He said he loved me, you know," said Anne, seemingly out of nowhere. "He pursued me for years, built a new church to have me." Her eyes wildly followed the faces that formed a sea of hostility around her. "What do you think? Do you believe a man who does what the King has done for me, could really hate me this much?"

She said no more. Her own trial would be in a few days, if one could call it a trial, and the verdict was a foregone conclusion. George might still have a chance, but that was unlikely. She wondered briefly why the King hated George so much, but it took only a moment to realise that, like all the others, it was Cromwell who wanted George among them.

"My brother must be suffering so," said Anne. She looked about to see if anyone were really listening. "He'll not be in lush apartments like these, will he? He'll be in a prison cell with few comforts."

One of the younger ladies spoke up and earned a glare from the others.

"I have it on good authority, Your Grace," she said, "that Viscount Rochford has a comfortable place. Lady Rochford has been sending him comforts, and paying for extra food."

She blushed a dark crimson, then dropped her gaze to her embroidery.

"Thank you for that," said Anne. "I am so pleased to know that his wife has not forsaken him, that Jane does not believe these lies. I often thought she envied our closeness; perhaps she did, but at least she does not accept the falsehoods. Thank you."

For the first time her thoughts turned to her sister-in-law, to Lady Jane Rochford, George's wife, and she was ashamed to admit that she had given her not a single thought until now. It had been an arranged match, but Jane and George had been content together. She must have been devastated by this, but Anne had not thought of her at all. How selfish that was; she hoped Jane would forgive her.

In her letter to the King, she had pleaded with him for a fair trial, a lawful trial, but she could see that was not the sort she would receive. And she finally realised, after telling herself that Henry was doing this to punish her, that he did mean it, that he intended her death. Once King Henry of England intended a thing, that thing would come to pass, no matter who had to suffer for it to happen.

She dressed with care for the trial, not wanting to appear overdressed or superior. Her clothing was plain, a black velvet gown with a crimson petticoat. She wore no jewellery, other than her wedding ring and she followed Master Kingston to the King's Hall within the Tower itself.

She looked about for George, presuming he was to be tried with her, but there was no sign of him as she took her place.

In the centre of the hall, a great scaffold had been erected and on it, in an elaborate chair, sat one of Anne's worst enemies, her uncle, the Duke of Norfolk. So another request of hers had gone unanswered, that she should be judged not by her enemies.

Henry must hate her! He had sent this man, who had plotted to bring her down, to arrest her and now he had sent this man to preside over the proceedings, proceedings upon which her life depended. She might as well submit her neck to the block here and now.

She mounted the platform and took the seat opposite her uncle. Her dark eyes wandered to the jury and she saw that each one an enemy, each one was a man who had always been against her, blamed her for Katherine's fall, blamed her for the separation of the church, for the bastardisation of the Princess Mary. Even Charles Brandon, the Duke of Suffolk and the King's brother-in-law, a man who despised Anne with all his soul, sat grave faced, his arms folded, his eyes filled with loathing.

There was but one who might be on her side in this, who might still care enough to fight for her – Lord Harry Percy, Earl of Northumberland, the man she had always loved. But why was he here, among her enemies? This must be some cruel jest of the King, to force Harry Percy of all people to sit with these men in judgment on her.

She scarcely recognised him, he looked so ill, so drawn and thin. His skin was of a shiny texture, tinted with yellow, his hair and beard dull and lacklustre. And as she watched him, she could see he did not want to be here. He shifted uncomfortably in his seat, his mouth a thin line of misery, and as he turned his head away, she saw the tears which gathered in his eyes.

She did not bother to ask herself again why the King now hated her so much, did not care to question why he would subject her to this further humiliation of having her former sweetheart sit in judgment on her. And some twisted need for vengeance made Henry want to punish Harry Percy as well, to force him to be here, to sit among her enemies.

Anne's memory showed her those first days at court, not so very long ago, when she had danced with Harry Percy, had courted him, kissed him, loved him. She remembered those secret meetings and how they had promised each other marriage, promised to belong to each other forever.

They could have been happy together, she and Harry, had the King not wanted her for himself, had he not been determined to have his own way in all things. And look what he had done, look to what he had brought those two young lovers.

The trial did not last long and Anne was not allowed to speak. There was no real evidence, only false statements, Mark Smeaton's confession which could well have been made under torture. If not, he may well have thought himself important that someone would think he was having intimate relations with the Queen. He was such a child in a lot of ways, a talented child who had no understanding of the real world.

Forced to sit and listen to the lies that were being told about her, forced to keep silent while those lies were accepted as truth, Anne fought against self pity. After the years of hearing lies which made her responsible for all the woes of the nation, she should be accustomed to them by now.

She opened her mouth to speak a few times to begin with, to refute the false evidence, but she was firmly told that any such interruption would result in her removal from the court.

She could only sit, helplessly, and shake her head in denial. The 'evidence' was not only ludicrous, ridiculous, laughable even, it was offensive. She had always been faithful to the King. She had not wanted him, had never loved him, but she had known no other man but him. And he knew it.

The verdict of all the men was 'guilty'; that came as no surprise and as her eyes met those of Harry Percy, her slowly shook his head, attempted a smile, then dropped his gaze to his trembling knees. She knew he had no choice but to agree. This was Henry's doing, this was what the King had ordered, and just like his forced marriage to Mary Talbot, no one defied the King.

When sentence was passed, Anne's heart jumped and she caught back a scream. She was to be taken to prison in the Tower and then, at the King's command, to the Green within the Tower, and there to be burned or beheaded, as shall please the King.

Burned. That was the word that assaulted her mind. It was the prescribed sentence for female traitors but, try as she would, she could think of no woman who had suffered that horrific death for the crime of treason. And she wondered if the man she had married could really see her screaming in agony as the flames caught her clothing and seared her flesh. But he would not see it, would he? He would make himself scarce, would want to know nothing about it, because that was what he did, that was how cowards behaved.

His beloved Anne, the woman he would love forever, the woman who was dearer to him than anyone or anything. She laughed shortly, then composed herself to give her speech, as it was the only speech she would be permitted to give.

"My Lord," she began. "I will not say your sentence is unjust, nor presume that my reasons can prevail against your convictions. I am willing to believe that you have sufficient reasons for what you have done, but then they must be other than those which have been produced in court, for I am clear of all the offences which you then laid to my charge. I have ever been a faithful wife to the King, though I do not say I have always shown him that humility which his goodness to me, and the honours to which he raised me, merited."

Her words were interrupted by a loud thud, as of something heavy falling, and she stopped and turned her gaze to the sound. Harry Percy had collapsed and lay unconscious upon the floor as several of the pages hurried to lift him and carry him out of the Hall.

Anne knew for certain this was all too much for him, knew too that his verdict had been forced upon him. So he did still care for her, as she still cared for him.

She continued her speech, lest someone use this interruption as an excuse to cut off her words before they could be spoken.

"I confess I have had jealous fancies and suspicions of him," she went on, "which I had not discretion enough, and wisdom, to conceal at all times. But God knows, and is my witness, that I have not sinned against him in any other way. Think not I say this in the hope to prolong my life, for He who saves from death has taught me how to die, and He will strengthen my faith. Think not, however, that I am so bewildered in my mind that I will not maintain my chastity as I have done all my life.

"I know these, my last words, will avail me nothing but for the justification of my chastity and honour. As for my brother and those others who are unjustly condemned, I would willingly suffer many deaths to deliver them, but since I see it so pleases the King, I shall willingly accompany them in death, with this assurance, that I shall lead an endless life with them in peace and joy, where I will pray to God for the King and for you, my Lords."

She was led away then, quickly, before she decided to say more and she could not avoid the sight of the axe, turned with its blade toward her, a sign of the guilty verdict.

In her apartments, she said nothing, only looked from the window to see the building of the scaffold upon which her friends would meet their end. But not her, not Anne. She might be tied to a stake with faggots piled around her feet. Those faggots would be lit and as the flames approached, as they crept stealthily toward the flammable fabric of her clothing, her flesh would be melted until it slid off her bones.

No! She could not bear it! Surely he would not do that, surely not, after everything they had been to each other. Beneath her breath, she cursed the King, cursed him to Hell; why had he not left her alone? She had never wanted to be Queen, she had never wanted to marry him, she had never loved him. True, she had been pleased by the break with Rome and was proud to be the cause of it, but not proud to have ousted Katherine.

She needed to be careful now, or her words would be reported and if she was heard to curse the King, she would have no chance of a less brutal death.

"Your Majesty." A soft voice caught her attention. "Forgive me for disturbing you, but I heard a rumour that I thought might bring some small peace."

It was one of the ladies sent in to report on her every word and Anne knew she should not trust her, but she seemed sincere. She spoke in whispers, so that only Anne would hear. Anne nodded.

"Go on," she said.

"The others say it would make you angry, but I fear you might worry about your sentence. I was told, from one in the King's household, that His Majesty had sent to France for an expert swordsman to carry out the sentence."

"A swordsman? So I am not to be burned." Those wretched tears were back, this time tears of relief. "When did he do this? The verdict has only this morning been given."

"It is said that His Majesty sent for him on the day you were arrested, Your Grace," she said. "I am sorry."

Anne had no reply for her. The entire charade was for the benefit of any who would say she had no fair trial. Henry had already decided on the outcome and the sentence, and nothing she said or did was ever going to change his mind.

***

When Harry opened his eyes, he found himself in a strange chamber surrounded by tapestry covered stone walls. The shape of the windows told him he was still in the Tower, likely the apartments of one of the Yeoman guards, but he had no idea how long he had been here.

Memories started to come back, memories he hoped were but bad dreams. He had to pronounce her guilty; it was what the tyrant wanted and he had no choice. Even if he had held out for a not guilty verdict, all it would have meant was Harry losing everything. It would have changed nothing for Anne, because the other jurors all said 'guilty', the others who had been carefully chosen. Harry was the only friend she had among them, and his friendship had availed her nothing.

He felt ashamed of himself, but what else could he have done? The King had only summoned him for the task to see what would happen; Harry was sure of that. It amused the royal humour to put him in this position.

He did not expect to faint, of course. He hoped to comfort her somehow by his presence, since he could not avoid the task, but all he had done was make a fool of himself.

He closed his eyes and prayed silently that they would not burn her. He could not tolerate the thought and if they did, he would be tempted to leap into the flames beside her. He could not bear for his lovely lady to be burned.

His eyes opened and he realised he was not alone. A page stood beside the bed, a goblet of wine in his hand.

"My Lord," he said. "Are you recovered?"

Harry managed a nod of his head, then he scrambled into a sitting position and reached for the wine.

"Thank you," he said.

The page left him alone with his thoughts, with his grief. Soon Anne would be dead, dead at the hand of a man who swore he would love her forever, and after only a few short years. Three years, that was all since the marriage. She had given him a beautiful daughter, even though she had miscarried of his sons, but three years? He had hardly given her time to breed those sons.

***

Anne was told she was to die at dawn on 18th May, just three days after her trial. The gentlemen accused with her had already met their deaths, but Anne was to have a scaffold built specially for her.

The initial sentence for those innocent men, that they be hanged until almost dead, cut down whilst still living and their entrails cut out and burned within their sight, had been commuted to beheading. Even Mark Smeaton, a lowly fellow, escaped that horrific end. It was Anne's only comfort as her fervent prayers and pleas had not saved them.

On the morning of her expected execution, she rose early, dressed with care in a grey damask gown over a crimson kirtle, an English hood covering her dark hair. Then she awaited the arrival of Archbishop Cranmer, who was ever her friend, to hear her final confession and give the Last Rites.

Rumours were brought to her that her marriage to the King had been annulled. Having failed to persuade Harry Percy to admit to a pre-contract with her, Henry had achieved his wish for an annulment by citing his previous relationship with her sister, Mary. Strange how that had never bothered his famous conscience when it suited him.

The bitterness that churned away inside her threatened to destroy her long before the swordsman arrived. She still could not grasp how she had come to this, from one day being Henry's beloved wife, his only love, to the next day wanting to consign her to oblivion, erase her from existence.

Cranmer struggled to contain his tears.

"I am so sorry, Your Grace," he said. "I had no option. I had to annul your marriage to the King. I thought it might save you, but alas it did nothing to help."

She reached out a hand to comfort him.

"I understand. What happened to your predecessor when he failed to give Henry what he demanded? I am to die; there is no need for you to join me."

Then she asked that he commend her to the King and hoped her words would reach him so that he would know for certain she was innocent, that he would know what a terrible sin he had committed against her.

"Commend me to His Majesty," she said. "And tell him that he has ever been constant in advancing me. From a private gentlewoman he made me a Marquess, from that he made me a Queen. Now he has no higher degree of honour left, he gives my innocence the crown of martyrdom as a saint in Heaven."

If King Henry asked for her words, Cranmer would convey them, and he would most certainly write them down so that the future would see them.

On her knees, Queen Anne Boleyn gave her last confession and in it she declared her innocence. If the King wished to learn otherwise, he would be disappointed.

Cranmer stayed with her until after noon, by which time she was becoming restless. She stood at the window, staring out and up at the sun. It was past noon; she should be dead by now, should be with the angels, for she had no fear of anything else. She had a good view of the scaffold, could see the straw ready to accept her head, ready to soak up the blood as it poured from her severed neck. But there was no coffin.

A little spark of something similar to hope caught at her heart. Perhaps the King had changed his mind, perhaps he had remembered the love he once had for her, or said he had for her. But that was unlikely, as he was eager to wed the Seymour and had already murdered Anne's friends and her brother.

She spun around to where the Archbishop still waited with her.

"Why do they not get on with it?" she asked him. Her question struggled to pass the ache in her throat, her vision was blurred with her tears.

"I was told I was to die this morning; I am prepared to die." She gestured to the window, beyond which she could see the scaffold awaiting her. "The scaffold is ready. Why do they delay?"

The sound of footsteps approaching startled her. At last! Finally they had come for her, finally she could have peace from this life.

But it was Sir William Kingston alone, and he came to tell her that the swordsman was delayed and would not arrive until the following day. Anne's sorrow at the news overwhelmed her.

***

Anne did not sleep that night. With but one night left, she felt it would be better spent in prayer and her most urgent prayer was that there would be no further delay. She also prayed that those innocent gentlemen who were unjustly condemned with her, were now awaiting her in Paradise. She looked forward to meeting with them again, to being able to express her fondness for them without fear that some enemy might be listening and reporting.

She thought about those words she had spoken to Henry Norris; they were careless words, words that her enemy could twist and use against her.

And poor Mark. She held no malice toward him for his false confession. He was a simple boy and he was likely in terror; she had felt some of that terror herself these past weeks and for him, the horror must have been greater. They likely promised him his freedom if he spoke as they wanted. She was grateful to the King for commuting his sentence to beheading at least, and she had heard the axeman who despatched him and her other friends was efficient at least.

Yet she had more to consider as she lay awake and she was not alone in that. She heard the whispered words of her ladies as they repeated the latest gossip from court. She was not the only one who did not sleep that night, for word had it that the King also stayed up, but it was not his conscience that bothered him this time.

"I was told by one of the grooms that His Majesty spent hours studying the plans for the scaffold," whispered a soft voice. "He wants to be sure there is no mistake, that the execution will be carried out precisely as he has it planned."

"Did he seem distressed?" asked a new voice.

"No, not in the least. He seemed to be enthralled with it, measuring and scrutinising each piece of the platform, each step up to it. My friend said he looked intense, as though he were measuring the stage for some entertainment. He said the King was displeased that the swordsman had not arrived on time and wanted to make certain that nothing else went wrong."

Anne thought she heard a catch in the woman's voice as she replied.

"I should not express an opinion, but that is terrible. He was supposed to have loved her so much, look what he did for her. How could he do this now? How could he treat her death like a carefully planned exhibition?"

"Word is that he is now saying he never loved her, that he was enchanted, possibly even bewitched. He is even saying that he was led astray by her charms. How could he?"

They were right; how could he? Only a few weeks ago he was still referring to her as his most beloved wife.

That was all she heard before she turned her face to the wall and shut off the sound, waited for the light to creep through the sky.

At last Cranmer returned to tell her it was time. Sir William Kingston was with him, ready to escort her to the scaffold, to take her last steps.

"I hear the swordsman is very good, Master Kingston," she said. Then she put her hands up to encircle her throat. "And I have a little neck."

Her silent prayers were for Harry. She had not dared to ask about his condition since he collapsed at her trial, but he did look ill. Who knew? It might be that he, too, would soon join her in Heaven.

Unlike her friends and her brother, Anne's execution would not be a public one o Tower Hill. Hers would be within the Tower grounds, on Tower Green, where only those invited were allowed to attend.

Kingston helped her up the steps and onto the scaffold, where she stood to address the crowd. There were her enemies, seated at the front, those same enemies who had willingly condemned her, Suffolk chief among them, his arms folded, a look of triumph on his face.

Her eyes swept over them. There was no sign of Harry and she wondered if he had been excused this sight, or if he was still too ill to attend. She knew he would not have willingly come here to witness her terrible end.

The faces formed a sea, but she could not sense its mood. As Queen, she had grown used to crowds watching her, staring at her, and often they were hostile, but still reverend. This crowd was different; this crowd had come to see her die and they were mostly silent. It was a stunned sort of silence and Anne did not fool herself that it was a sympathetic one. She knew it was because they could not quite believe that a Queen of England was to suffer such a death.

She felt tears gathering, felt a lump in her throat that would likely stop her words and she could not have that. She fought against the need for self pity, fought against those tears; she would be remembered throughout history as the Queen who went to her unjust execution with the dignity of a Queen.

She swallowed the bunch of tears in her throat and began her speech, the last words she would ever speak. She knew that her marriage to the King had been annulled, that her little Elizabeth had been declared a bastard, and that the King could easily have spared her and still had his Jane Seymour.

She had many words she would have liked to say to Henry, but she was afraid. He could easily change this merciful form of execution to that of having her burnt alive; he could do more harm to her daughter if she did not make him sound like the most wonderful man who ever lived. It was what he believed himself to be, but there were those she would leave behind who would suffer for the truth.

She raised her voice and began to speak.

"Good Christian people," she said, "I have not come here to preach a sermon. I have come here to die, for according to the law and by the law, I am judged to die. Therefore I will speak nothing against it. I am come hither to accuse no man, nor to speak of that whereof I am accused and condemned to die, but I pray God save the King and send him long to reign over you, for a gentler nor a more merciful prince was there never, and to me he was ever a good, a gentle and sovereign lord.

"And if any person will meddle in my cause, I require them to judge the best. And thus I take my leave of the world and of you all and I heartily desire you all to pray for me."

She wondered if anyone would note the sarcasm in her praise of the King. Her words could be taken either way and that was her intent.

Two of her ladies stepped forward to take her mantle and Anne removed her hood and let her dark tresses fall about her shoulders for the briefest time, before she gathered them beneath a white cap to keep them out of the way of the sword.

The swordsman asked forgiveness, which she freely gave and she paid him his due, then she knelt in the straw and prayed to Jesus to accept her soul, but her hearing betrayed her as she turned her head to see where the swordsman stood.

He, seeing this, asked his assistant to hand him his sword and as her eyes followed the assistant, the swordsman struck.

Anne's ladies ran to gather up her remains and wrap them in linen, then they looked about urgently for a coffin that was not there. Nobody had bothered to order such a thing, no coffin for the Queen of England.

An arrow box was brought and the remains of Queen Anne Boleyn were placed inside and carried to the chapel of St Peter ad Vincula within the Tower, where they were buried in an unmarked grave.

CHAPTER SEVENTEEN
The Aftermath

News of Queen Anne's death cheered the Princess Mary more than anything else could have. The Concubine was dead! Mary's father had finally realised that he had been bewitched, entranced by her wiles into casting aside Mary's mother and Mary with her. It was Anne's fault she had been banished from court and now she was gone, Mary felt sure the King would welcome his daughter back and even restore her to her former position as the only legitimate heir to the throne.

Elizabeth was the bastard, not Mary. He had annulled his marriage to the Concubine and in so doing had declared Elizabeth illegitimate. It would not be long before those foreign princes would come courting Mary once more.

The King had shown his contempt for the Concubine by getting himself betrothed to another the very next day after her demise. That should tell the world that he was admitting to his mistake in joining with her.

The King had already chosen a new wife, a good Catholic woman who would help him restore the true church. She felt confident now in once again writing to her father, congratulating him on his coming marriage and begging to be allowed back to court.

She made no mention of Anne. She was unsure about his feelings on that subject and his anger was easily aroused.

The letter was carefully worded and was delivered to the King that same day, but the King's reply dismayed his daughter. Still, he insisted that she sign the Oath that recognised him as the head of the church.

So it was not the Concubine who had wanted this; it was Henry himself. Mary had always believed it was Anne who insisted on this, Anne who wanted Mary to yield to the heresy of the Church of England, but it seemed she was wrong. And if she was wrong, if the King still insisted on recognition as head of this new church, Mary's hopes that he would return to the fold of Rome were in vain.

At court, Henry allowed his new Queen Jane to read the letter from his daughter. He was very pleased with Jane. She was meek, obedient and had few opinions of her own, unlike that other one. She would give him sons, he was sure of it.

Now she rested her hand on his knee, leaned forward and kissed him, a gentle, affectionate kiss that would blossom into passion later, in her bedchamber.

"Would it be so very bad to allow your daughter back at court?" she said softly. "She has done nothing save defend her mother and her own beliefs."

Henry's mood changed, as it often did, and he threw her hand from him and scowled at her.

"I'd advise you not to meddle in my affairs, Madam," he said angrily. "Remember what became of your predecessor. Remember Anne."

***

Harry Percy stayed in his bedchamber for a month following Anne's execution. He took to his bed, both to soothe his continuing illness and his grief. He could not believe that Anne was gone and worse, that he had played a part in her going. He had no choice, he knew that and most importantly, so did she. She had even given him an encouraging smile, but that did nothing to assuage his guilt.

Still he hated himself, still he would have done almost anything to be able to join her. But Harry felt sure that day was not so very far away. This illness, whatever it was, had been growing worse for years and after these events, he had neither the strength nor the will to recover.

Returning to the north, he settled at Wressle Castle, another of his estates in Yorkshire. He intended to stay there throughout the summer, hope to live out what remained of his life in seclusion with his guilt.

News had a habit of reaching him, whether he wanted to hear it or not. It seemed the King was still going ahead with his plans to dissolved all the monasteries, not only the smaller ones. Anne had quarrelled with Cromwell about that, had wanted the money and income gained from their dissolution to be given to the poor, to charities and to education. Cromwell wanted it to swell the King's coffers and if Cromwell wanted it, it was certain that the King also wanted it.

There would be civil war over this, Harry was sure of it, but he was too ill and too despondent to care. Yet he was forced to care when, after returning from London, he received a visit from Robert Aske, the lawyer who was organising and leading a pilgrimage to London. There had already been one uprising in Lincolnshire in an effort to persuade the King to restore the monasteries. It had failed, of course it had.

Trying to persuade King Henry to do anything was a waste of time and ultimately, a waste of human lives. Such rebellions always ended in trials for treason, trials that were a foregone conclusion, just like Anne's.

Now, this Robert Aske was here in Harry's home and he had a good idea of what he wanted. Harry knew well that his own mother and brothers were sympathetic to the pilgrimage, but they needed him, the Earl of Northumberland and head of the family, to give credence and manpower to their cause.

Aske was shown into Harry's bedchamber, where he greeted him still wearing his nightgown, and with the windows covered in heavy drapes from the night before.

"Master Aske," said Harry. "Please sit and be quick. I am too ill for unnecessary civility."

"As I see, My Lord," Aske replied. "I am sorry to see it. I see you will be able to do little for the right and just cause which we represent, yet your name alone could be the difference between success and failure."

"My name, Sir?" said Harry. He gave a short, derisive laugh. "My name will do nothing save anger the King. Do you not know that he hates me?"

Aske shook his head.

"I am sure you are wrong, My Lord."

"Do not patronise me! Did the King not tear from me the only woman I ever loved? Did he not force me into a marriage with a woman I despised and who despised me? Did he not force me to be among those enemies of my love who condemned her?"

"I see your bitterness, My Lord, but surely that is even more reason for your opposition to his plan."

"Even if I were not so ill, even if I were stupid enough to oppose this tyrant King, I could not support your cause."

"Why not? Your brother and your mother..."

"I care nothing for them. I cannot support your cause because I do not believe in it. I think that the only good thing our beloved King ever did was to break us away from the oppression of Rome. I will support him in that, if in nothing else." He took a sip from his goblet, looking at his guest over the rim. "Now, please leave me in peace."

"Will you at least relinquish command of the marches into the hands of your brothers?"

"How would that be different from offering my support? I'll do nothing to support you and your cause."

"But your mother, your brothers..."

"My brothers are fools. I have seen nothing of them for so long, I can scarcely remember when. I intend to leave them nothing on my death, which will likely not be far off. Now leave, before I have you thrown out."

Harry returned to his bed and his intention to sleep the rest of his life away, but he was not to be given that privilege. Later that day, another lawyer arrived.

"William Stapleton, My Lord," said the visitor with a bow. "At your service."

Harry lifted his head and stared at him, but his only thought was to wonder why he could not be left alone to die in peace. The pain in his stomach grew worse with every interruption, keeping him from his sleep and making his anger fierce and dangerous.

"At my service?" he said, pushing himself into a sitting position. "Get me some wine and some for yourself if you will. Then tell me what you want and get out."

Stapleton handed him the wine, but took none for himself.

"I come from Master Aske," he began, but Harry put up a hand to stop him.

"Then you can have nothing to say that I might want to hear," he said.

"Please listen, My Lord, for your own benefit."

"My benefit? Joining my family in committing treason is now for my benefit?"

"Master Aske sent me as a matter of urgency. His followers are after your head and they will have it if you stay here. You are in danger, and I come only to escort you to York."

"What is in York save more of your traitors?"

"A monastery where you will be safe. Please, My Lord. Master Aske and I have no wish to harm you. You must trust us."

Harry rolled over and pulled the covers up over his head.

"Go away," he said.

"No, My Lord, I will not leave. I have an armed guard with me, ready to take you to York."

Many voices shouting came through the open window and Master Stapleton went to look down, where he saw familiar faces.

"My Lord," he said, turning back to the bed. "There are men outside. They want revenge because you refuse to support them. You must trust me."

Harry was too ill to argue. He had remained loyal to the King, but not for his own beliefs, not really. It was what Anne believed to be right and he kept her wishes out of duty to her memory.

He wanted nothing more than to end his life, but he had no wish to end it at the mercy of an angry rebel brandishing an axe. He had little choice but to allow his guest to help him dress and lead him to safety.

***

Harry returned to Newington Green in the New Year. He had seen enough of monks, heard enough of chanting, and there was always the danger that the King would send his army to arrest them all. Harry did not want to be involved.

The rebellion that Robert Aske had wanted him to join had failed, which came as no surprise to Harry. They had called it the Pilgrimage of Grace, but Harry saw nothing graceful about it. It was a rebellion, no matter what they chose to call it.

There were forty thousand pilgrims, forty thousand who had gathered up some nuns and monks who had been displaced and restored them to their monastery and nunnery homes, having ousted the King's new tenants.

That was a brave move, if a foolhardy one, but forty thousand people met with the Duke of Norfolk's seven thousand. Harry's father-in-law, the Earl of Shrewsbury, was there as well. That was a man he would always loathe; he was as much to blame for Harry's miserable life as the King. He had forced his daughter into the marriage, then, instead of leaving them to sort out their differences and try to make something of it, he had interfered and sent servants to spy on them.

Harry was sorry the man had escaped from this meeting with his life. Norfolk, too, should have perished.

But they knew they were vastly outnumbered, so they made an agreement with the pilgrims. According to what the monks in York had told Harry, Norfolk and Shrewsbury had made certain promises on behalf of the King, enough to make Robert Aske disperse his followers, send them back to their homes.

They should never have trusted the King's men. Harry knew that, so why did they not know it? He would not have trusted them, would never have believed that the King would compromise, would go back on his actions, admit he was wrong. He was the King; he was never wrong. Henry sincerely believed that every thought that entered his head was God speaking to him and how could God be wrong?

Once the pilgrims had gone, the leaders were arrested and charged with treason. Harry might have found it amusing, had he not been too ill to care. Two of those charged were his own brothers, Sir Thomas Percy and Sir Ingram Percy.

Ingram was too young to know what he was doing. He likely only followed Thomas and now they were both in danger of being charged with treason. Harry wondered for a brief moment whether everyone close to him was destined to be executed.

But Thomas' end was much harsher than that French swordsmen who took the life of Anne. He suffered that ghastly death of being hanged, cut down while still alive, having his genitals and entrails cut out of him before he was sliced into quarters and taken to various parts of the country to be displayed as a traitor. His head would be mounted on a spike somewhere for all to see.

Harry's brother, his own flesh and blood. His mother was pardoned, as she had no serious part in the rebellion and for that Harry was grateful. He cared little for her, but it would be assumed she would have been obeying his commands, as the Earl and head of the family. He had to disown her, in order to save himself.

He heard that his youngest brother, Ingram, had been imprisoned in the Tower with no definite date for either his execution or his release. Harry should plead with the King for him; he was his elder brother, the Earl of Northumberland, but he could not bring himself to care enough.

Robert Aske and some of the other leaders had been sentenced to be hung in chains. That was a horrendous death, to be hung from the castle walls, no food or drink, left to soil themselves for however long it took them to die. Perhaps Thomas had the better end; it was terrifying and agonising, but it was quicker than Aske's.

And all these men really wanted was to be allowed to follow their own consciences. Harry wondered if that was a privilege that would ever be permitted to any man.

It was a long journey to Newington Green from York, not one that Harry's health was really good enough for. He tried to sleep during the journey, but it was hot inside the carriage and the uneven roads were not conducive to rest. Every bump in the road hurt his insides till he wanted to scream out in agony.

Every time he did sleep, though, his dreams showed him his childhood, when he and his brothers were friends. They would play together in the grounds of Alnwick Castle, they would pretend to be Robin Hood or King Arthur, Sir Lancelot; they would even find the Holy Grail and hide it somewhere. He woke wondering if that cup they had stolen from the kitchens was still where they had hidden it.

His eyes were filled with tears, tears he had not been able to shed during his waking hours. Those childhood memories were hidden behind a wall of bitterness, before he was sent to serve Thomas Wolsey, the great Cardinal, before he had met Anne, before he had fallen in love. He had known dreams then, dreams of a future with a wife who loved him, of children who would play happily in those same grounds where he and his brothers had played. They might even find that 'Holy Grail', if it were still there.

But Anne had been too beautiful for him, too enchanting for him. The King had wanted her, so Harry was forced to marry a woman who hated him for loving someone else.

He could hardly blame her. Imagine how he would have felt, knowing that it was Mary who loved someone else. But he could not imagine that, because it was always Anne that he wanted.

The King had ruined all their lives, Harry's, Mary's, Anne's, and now he was free to ruin others.

***

The summer heat warmed the air both outside and in. Harry tried to sleep, but the heat was too intense and he threw off his nightclothes in an attempt to cool himself. His body was emaciated now, as he had eaten little for weeks.

It hurt to eat, but his stomach was distended, almost the shape of a pregnant belly, but yellow.

The pain was unbearable, caused him to scream out in his sleep or out of it. The whites of his eyes were yellow and he knew his mind was failing. He could scarcely tell his dreams from reality any more; he would open his eyes and think Anne was there, would think they were still young and in love.

She was so lovely. Not in any way that would turn heads, but when she spoke, when she laughed, there was never anything so beautiful. It was that laugh, that joy of life, that attracted the tyrant.

That morning he had a brief visit from Richard Layton, a representative of the King, likely sent to confirm that Harry really was dying. He had willed his lands to the King, personally, and the monarch likely wanted to be sure he would get them sooner rather than later.

Harry could hardly remember why he had left his lands to that King who had destroyed his life. He thought it was done in the hope that Anne would gain something from it, as she was still Henry's beloved wife at the time. But later, he had no idea why he left it as such. It hardly mattered.

Layton stayed but a few minutes, and his presence made it necessary for Harry to cover himself, but he made no effort to rise from his bed.

"I came to see how you fare, My Lord," said Layton. "The King was anxious."

"I'll just wager he was," said Harry. "Well, you can tell him he will soon get his hands on my property. As you see, it cannot be long before I go to join my beloved." Harry paused to cough, then his yellow eyes looked up at his visitor. "Please tell him I said that," he added. "I want him to know that she was loved by me, if not by him."

Layton's eyes opened wide in shock and he took a step back, colliding with the chair behind him. He had no intention of telling the King any such thing.

"I will leave you in peace, My Lord," he said quickly. "I wish you well."

"You'll not have your wish."

He slept some more, his only prayer that he should soon leave this world. If there was a purgatory, as the Roman Church taught, Harry was sure he had already suffered it.

He thought he had dozed again, that he was still asleep and dreaming, but this vision was too real for that. It was Anne, but it could not be Anne. Anne was dead, her beautiful head sliced from her body by order of her own husband.

Her hand reached toward him and he lifted his own to take it. He felt her soft fingers entwine around his own, felt them as he had all those years ago when they thought they had a future.

It *was* Anne and as he sat up to reach her, his pain and his sickness disappeared. He felt as young and fit as he had then, when first he laid eyes on her.

She smiled, her eyes full of love, and pulled him to his feet.

Letter by Anne Boleyn to King Henry VIII 6 May 1536 – This letter was apparently found among the papers of Thomas Cromwell, but its authenticity is in dispute. It is doubtful that the King ever saw it.

Your grace's displeasure and my imprisonment are things so strange to me, that what to write, or what to excuse, I am altogether ignorant. Whereas you send to me (willing me to confess a truth and so obtain your favour), by such a one, whom you know to be mine ancient professed enemy, I no sooner received this message by him, than I rightly conceived your meaning; and if, as you say, confessing a truth indeed may procure my safety, I shall with all willingness and duty, perform your duty. But let not your grace ever imagine that your poor wife will be brought to acknowledge a fault, where not so much as a thought ever proceeded. And to speak a truth, never a prince had wife more loyal in all duty, and in all true affection, than you have ever found in Anne Bulen – with which name and place I could willingly have contented myself, if God and your grace's pleasure had been so pleased. Neither did I at any time so far forget myself in my exaltation or received queenship, but that I always looked for such alteration as I now find; for the ground of my preferment being on no surer foundation than your grace's fancy, the least alteration was fit and sufficient (I knew) to draw that fancy to some other subject.

You have chosen me from low estate to be your queen and companion, far beyond my desert or desire; if, then, you found me worthy of such honour, good your grace, let not any light fancy or bad counsel of my enemies withdraw your princely favour from me; neither let that stain – that unworthy stain – of a disloyal heart towards your good grace ever cast so foul a blot on me, and on the infant princess your daughter.

Try me, good king, but let me have a lawful trial, and let not my sworn enemies sit as my accusers and as my judges; yea, let me receive an open trial, for my truth shall fear no open shame. Then you shall see either my innocence cleared, your suspicions and conscience satisfied, the ignominy and slander of the world stopped, or my guilt openly declared. So that, whatever God and you may determine of, your grace may be freed from an open censure; and my offense being so lawfully proved, your grace may be at liberty, both before God and man, not only to execute worthy punishment on me as an unfaithful wife but to follow your affection already settled on that party for whose sake I am now as I am, whose name I could some while since have pointed unto – your grace being not ignorant of my suspicions therein. But if you have already determined of me, and that not only my death, but an infamous slander must bring your the joying of your desired happiness, then I desire of God that he will pardon your great sin herein, and likewise my enemies, the instruments thereof; and that he will not call you to a strait account for your unprincely and cruel usage of me at his general judgment-seat, where both you and myself must shortly appear; and in whose just judgment, I doubt not (whatsoever the world may think of me), mine innocence shall be openly known and sufficiently cleared.

My last and only request shall be, that myself only bear the burden of your grace's displeasure, and that it may not touch the innocent souls of those poor gentlemen, whom, as I understand, are likewise in strait imprisonment for my sake. If ever I have found favour in your sight – if ever the name of Anne Bulen have been pleasing in your ears – then let me obtain this request; and so I will leave to trouble your grace any further, with mine earnest prayer to the Trinity to have your grace in his good keeping, and to direct you in all your actions. From my doleful prison in the Tower, the 6th May.

Anne Boleyn's Speech, on hearing the verdict against her:

My lords, I will not say your sentence is unjust, nor presume that my reasons can prevail against your convictions. I am willing to believe that you have sufficient reasons for what you have done; but then they must be other than those which have been produced in court, for I am clear of all the offences which you then laid to my charge. I have ever been a faithful wife to the King, though I do not say I have always shown him that humility which his goodness to me, and the honours to which he raised me, merited. I confess I have had jealous fancies and suspicions of him, which I had not discretion enough, and wisdom, to conceal at all times. But God knows, and is my witness, that I have not sinned against him in any other way. Think not I say this in the hope to prolong my life, for He who saveth from death hath taught me how to die, and He will strengthen my faith. Think not, however, that I am so bewildered in my mind as not to lay the honour of my chastity to heart now in mine extremity, when I have maintained it all my life long, much as ever queen did. I know these, my last words, will avail me nothing but for the justification of my chastity and honour. As for my brother and those others who are unjustly condemned, I would willingly suffer many deaths to deliver them, but since I see it so pleases the King, I shall willingly accompany them in death, with this assurance, that I shall lead an endless life with them in peace and joy, where I will pray to God for the King and for you, my lords.

Anne Boleyn's Speech at her Execution:

Good Christian people, I have not come here to preach a sermon; I have come here to die, for according to the law and by the law I am judged to die, and therefore I will speak nothing against it. I am come hither to accuse no man, nor to speak of that whereof I am accused and condemned to die, but I pray God save the King and send him long to reign over you, for a gentler nor a more merciful prince was there never, and to me he was ever a good, a gentle and sovereign lord.

And if any person will meddle of my cause, I require them to judge the best. And thus I take my leave of the world and of you all, and I heartily desire you all to pray for me. 19ᵗʰ May 1536

Author's Note:

Anne Boleyn is one historical figure who most people recognise without thought. Volumes have been written about her, historians still argue over her, and there is even a faction which believes she was guilty of the charges for which she was condemned. I think that is rubbish.

In his confession, Mark Smeaton named various places and dates when he slept with her. Anne was never at those places on those dates; she was elsewhere and with the King, so he knew perfectly well Mark's confession was false. I doubt that mattered to him; he was, as always, about to get his own way and that was all that concerned him.

I have heard many different opinions about her, and that is what they are – opinions. I have heard that she and King Henry were very much in love, I have heard that she manipulated him to become Queen, I have heard that she deliberately set out to climb to those heights.

If Anne's letter to the King from her prison in the Tower is genuine, it is interesting to note that she says, quite clearly, that she never asked to be

Queen, that she was quite content to be simply Anne Boleyn, gentlewoman. It is that very fact that convinces me of the letter's authenticity.

But let us look at those opinions more closely. Anne was in love with Lord Henry Percy, she wanted to marry him, she believed she would marry him. For a brief time, she was happy.

It is said that she despised Cardinal Wolsey for the rest of his life because he separated her from Percy. She might well have hated him for the public way in which he did so, but he was acting on the orders of the King and she came to know that.

George Cavendish, Wolsey's servant, in his 'Life of Cardinal Wolsey', states quite clearly that this was the reason, although nobody but Wolsey knew it at the time. Some historians have questioned this, but Cavendish was there. His account is an eye witness account and I prefer to believe someone who was present, than someone who questions more than four hundred years later.

When Anne discovered it was the King who refused her marriage, because he had his eye on her, is it likely that she ever loved him? I think not. Henry VIII was a tyrant who had too much power for his own good and could twist anything into treason if it suited him. This is evidenced by his treatment of Anne herself at the end.

She could not get away from him and I have never believed that she refused to have sex with him to keep him interested. I believe she did that because she simply did not want him, hoped he would go away.

Did he love her? He divorced the very royal Katherine of Aragon, risking war with Spain, banished his own daughter and stripped her of her status, risked his soul (according to his time and his own beliefs) by breaking away from the Church of Rome, all so he could have Anne Boleyn. Then he discarded her after a mere three years of marriage. He annulled his marriage to her, citing his previous relationship with her sister (which, of course, he knew about when he married her) so there was no reason for her to die. There could be no charge of adultery if they were never legally married. Despite that, he anticipated her death with as much lust as he'd once had for her body. He spent the night before her execution poring over plans for the scaffold, he went out hunting and dancing while she awaited death, he got himself betrothed the day after her execution. Doesn't sound to me like a man who loved her, or who had ever loved her.

When Henry's fifth wife, Catherine Howard, was found guilty of adultery, he was devastated.

He thought he had finally found a woman who loved him, who was pure, only to discover she was writing love letters and giving herself freely to his servant, Thomas Culpepper. Then he discovered she was no virgin when he married her.

He was heartbroken then, so why was he not heartbroken when he discovered the same of Anne? Probably because he knew very well the charges were false.

Once he had discovered how much more power and wealth he could have by being the head of his own church, he turned on his closest friends to achieve it. When he wanted to be rid of Anne, he implicated Sir Henry Norris, a man who had been his close friend for years. He must have known he wasn't guilty, but so what? It suited the King for him to die, so that was his fate.

I think Anne is one of the most tragic figures in history, an innocent victim of a spoilt King who would not accept there was something he could not have.

That is my opinion; it is not fact, it is how I see it.

Thank you for reading For the Love of Anne. I hope you have enjoyed it and if you have, please leave a review on the Amazon website. Please also consider my other books: